# ALBY'S
## LETTERS TO HENRY

# ALBY'S
## LETTERS TO HENRY
### (from Mull)

Compiled by Iain Tennant       Illustrated by W. D. Smith

Bene Factum Publishing

Published by Bene Factum Publishing Ltd

Hardback edition ISBN 1-903071-09-7 (978-1-903071-09-0)
Published 2006

Paperback edition ISBN 1-903071-14-3 (978-1-903071-14-4)
Published 2007

By
Bene Factum Publishing Limited
10 Elm Quay Court
Nine Elms Lane
London SW8 5DE

A CIP catalogue record of this is available from the British Library

Text reproduction by Carnegie Book Production, Lancaster LA1 4SL
Cover design by Fielding Design, London SW15 1AZ
Printed in Great Britain by Biddles, King's Lynn PE30 4LS

# Prologue

During the Christmas holidays of 1984, a four-year-old grandson, called Henry, threw a tantrum one evening while staying with his grandparents. He refused to stay in bed, and his parents could do nothing with him. The noise got so bad that Henry's grandfather asked permission to try to quieten his grandson. Permission was granted.

Grandpa entered Henry's room with caution. As he passed the door, he got a Dinky toy amidships and was told to "go away".

To this day, Grandpa does not know what made him say it, but he told Henry to beware of ALBY who was under the bed.

"Who is ALBY?" asked the little boy.

"A great big Stag", said his grandfather, not knowing why he said that either!

Henry looked under the bed, and as he did so, Grandpa withdrew. All was quiet.

Ten minutes later, Grandpa went back to the room. Henry was asleep with his thumb in his mouth, leaning out of the bed as if looking for ALBY. At that moment Granny shouted for Grandpa to come to the telephone. Henry woke up, and flung another toy at Grandpa, shouting more abuse. The telephone call broke the spell, and Henry didn't go to sleep for ages.

Some weeks later, Grandpa went to stay with Henry, his Dad and his Mum. Soon after arriving, while Grandpa was talking to Henry's Mum, he felt a little hand squeezing his. When he looked down, he saw Henry, who said rather solemnly –

"Grandpa, where's Alby?"

Maybe that will help the reader to understand the reason for the fantasies that follow. They take place in Mull because Mull is where Henry spends most of his holidays, and he, like his family and many others, loves the island very much.

From 21st February, 1985, Henry received a letter every Saturday for fifty-two weeks signed by Alby, or one of his animal friends, giving him news of Stagland in Mull.

It is these letters that have become known in Henry's family as "Alby's Letters to Henry (from Mull)".

# Acknowledgements

Alby is most grateful to all who have encouraged him to send these letters to Henry. They tell the story of Ben More Stagland throughout the year.

Alby is particularly grateful to Ada Fersen for typing each letter two, three or even four times and for her patience with his bad spelling, bad punctuation and bad English!

Alby wishes to thank Bill Smith for the trouble he has taken to get to know all his friends in Stagland. Bill's illustrations will greatly help the reader to understand life on Ben More.

Finally, Alby wishes to thank Henry's Mum and Dad for reading the letters to Henry each week, and Henry's Mummy's Mummy and Daddy who gave him a big hand in writing the letters.

# The Alby Fund

After a 21 year absence this facsimile edition of Alby is being reproduced for a number of reasons

- I want to introduce a new generation of readers to the same joys of Alby that I had when I was young
- Alby addresses a number of important issues that are as significant today as they were when the letters were first written
- It is also published in memory of Alby's creator my grandfather, Iain Tennant, who died this summer. He was elighted that Alby was to reappear and gave his wholehearted support to the project.

This project is not for personal profit. I have established The Alby Fund to which the proceeds of this book will go.

The fund sets out to look after the people of the Ross of Mull (Alby's home) and is managed by myself and two other friends who also want to help benefit Mull.

Henry Cheape
December 2006

# Contents

"These letters are published not only for Henry and his friends who have the good fortune to be brought up to love the hills and all God's creatures that live there, but also for other young people who may never have the chance to go to the hills, but might like to dream their way there".

Iain Tennant
1919–2006

# Letter No. 1 *from Alby to Henry*

TELEPHONE
STAGLAND 303

SOMEWHERE ON THE ISLE OF MULL
ARGYLL
SCOTLAND
21st February

Hello how are you Henry?

I hope you are being a good boy because, when you are not, my next year's horns stop growing and that hurts me very much, especially as my next year's horns feel like being very good ones. I may even be a Royal! My last year's horns, with their ten points are very loose now and will soon fall off.

I am writing from high up on the hills of Mull, on the top of Ben More, looking across at Iona and Staffa and Ulva, but I have been spending the Winter down near the sea with my chums. It is not so cold there and from time to time I can pinch a few turnips to eat off one of the farmers.

It is such a lovely day today, I thought I would take a wee walk to see if the whole Island is still here – it is! That stupid grandson of mine, Rory, the nobber, has come with me but no one else. Rory is a complete idiot and keeps thinking he smells horrible hunters crawling up the hill after his blood – as if they would! He's not worth more than a myxie rabbit.

The hinds have had a bad time. The hunters never stop shovelling shots at them, and many have been turned into sausages (hope I'll never be a sausage). The other day poor old Morag (she's the oldest hind-In the herd, with floppy ears and no this-years-baby) smelt the hunters coming up the hill and hardly had time to get out of her brackeny bed before the shots' started bang-banging all around her hoofs. However, she got away with a scratch on her tail and a burn on the top of her left ear. She is Rory's mother but I don't think they get on too well. You see, Rory was always a spoilt little boy and now he is two years old, he has joined the stag-herd, so Morag doesn't see him very often.

*… Two old men crawling through the heather with their bottoms in the air …*

At this moment Rory is running round and round in circles, saying he can smell the enemy – I'm going to trip him up soon! Oh, no! wait a minute, he's quite right – I smell hunters as well. I see them now, two old men crawling through the heather with their bottoms in the air and looking like sea serpents in stalkers hats. They think we can't see them.

We are out of season now so they shouldn't harm us, but Rory is in such a stew, I think we had better get back into the birch trees at the bottom of the hill.

Be good, Henry. We're off down the hill at the gallop – I'll post this express by Golden Eagle Post when I get to the bottom.

Will write again next week.

Your pal,

Alby

*Golden Eagle Post*

# Letter No. 2 *from Alby to Henry*

TELEPHONE
STAGLAND 303

SOMEWHERE ON THE ISLE OF MULL
ARGYLL
SCOTLAND
28th February

Hello Henry

I hope my last letter reached you safely by the FAST-SWOOPING-GOLDEN-EAGLE POST.

You will remember that I ended by telling you that Rory had smelt horrible hunters so we had decided to go back to the Birch trees near the bottom of the hill. It was just as well we did because those horrible hunters were poachers and nearly nicked Ronnie the Roe Deer only a few hundred yards from where we were standing – but they missed.

We got back to the rest of the boys who were browsing in the frozen ferns. Deer are so much more sensible than you people. 1n the deer forest stags keep to themselves except in autumn when it is love-making time. The stags don't have to bother with female gossip while resting or munching. Come to think of it, the hinds don't have to bother about cooking our dinner and making our beds and looking after us all day either!

Anyway, I settled down for the evening after a small meal of dry-frozen last year's grass, and Rory bounded off to play with some of his rough schoolboy friends. Out of my left eye I could

*Gorkie, the old cock grouse*

see the hinds way up the hill, with the setting sun and the dark blue sky of evening behind them. Old Morag would have been up there somewhere.

As it got dark some friends came out for a blether. First Gorkie; the old Cock Grouse. He has been here for years and years, but he sadly lost his wife, Jemima, a wee while ago when Freddie the Fox suddenly jumped out from behind a rock and chopped her head off: Gorkie is busy looking for another wife but he tells me they are few and far between. He is a wise old bird with much experience of being shot at and missed – he knows just when to turn. He tells me that it is becoming very difficult to bring up grouse babies because they live on insects which fall from the heather buds just after the grouse babies come out of their eggs. Because of all the horrible things you folk put on your crops to make them grow and the rain which is dirty from the smoke out of your factory chimneys on the mainland, many of these little insects are killed and that means no food for the poor grouse babies, and that means the grouse babies die, and that means there are very few lady grouse for Gorkie to marry!

Gorkie thinks that very soon hunters won't be allowed to shoot grouse birds any more because there will be so few of them left. The horrible hunters will be very angry but it will be good for us, Henry, because when we are being hunted, the grouse birds watch over us and whenever they see the horrible hunters, they fly off shouting 'Go back, Go back, Go back', and then we know it's time for us to start smelling the air and keeping our eyes open.

After an hour or so, Gorkie flew off to his rock near the top of the hill.

A little while later, Olly the owl floated by in the gloaming, and when he saw me, he turned round and came back, settling on the branch of a birch tree just above my horns. 'Twit-a-wit-a-woo,' he said. Owl language is very difficult to understand – rather like Chinese to you – but it's worth trying to understand because ally and his friends are interesting people. They sleep all day and see nothing but are awake all night and see everything! Olly told me that he had been watching Freddie the Fox, at dead of night, pinching farmer McTavish's chickens out of his farmyard. He told me Freddie just chopped the chickens' heads off and only ate the heads, leaving all the rest of the chicken on the floor. Then, at other times, Freddie would chase the ewes on the hill but they were usually too crafty to be caught. Sometimes Freddie could be seen even looking for grouse birds to eat with chicken-head sauce.

Freddie the Fox is becoming an enemy of all our friends so I asked Olly to tell Freddie that we would all like him much more if he would stick to rats and mouses for his meals. Olly was very angry and said that those were his food and there weren't enough for anyone else and certainly not for Freddie. There was then a 'Twit-a-wit-a-woo', and he flew off into the dark in a bait.

After he had gone, Bunnie the brown Rabbit came out of his hole and started munching a small green bit of grass that must belong to next season and had come out of the ground early – but more of Bunny in my next as I must go to sleep now so that I will be up in time to give this letter to Golden Eagle Post in the morning.

My horns are hurting very much – I think one of them will fall off very soon. Please be as good as you can, Henry, because the better you are, the less my horns hurt.

Your old Pal,

Alby

# Letter No. 3 from Alby to Henry

TELEPHONE
STAGLAND 303

SOMEWHERE ON THE ISLE OF MULL
ARGYLL
SCOTLAND
7th March

Hello Henry,

You know, I was just thinking that I never know when you get my letter, so it might be a good idea if you shouted out, 'HELLO ALBY' as soon as Dad or Mum has read out the beginning of my letter, where it says 'Hello Henry'. Shout back, out of the window as loud as you can so that I can hear it on the top of Ben More.

Try it now and see how it sounds. OK?

Remember, at the end of last week's letter, Brown Bunnie had just come out to talk to me while he guzzled green grass shoots. I told you I would tell you more about him. There is not much to tell. Poor bunnies, they get nasty Myxie and come out in big spots by the time autumn comes, and most of them die – or are eaten by Freddie or are used as petrol to make the engines of the Golden Eagle Post work. Anyway, I think I've talked enough about my friends – Old-Morag-the-Hind and Ronnie-the-Roe and Gorkie-the-Grouse and Olly-the-Owl and Freddie-the-Fox and Brown-Bunnie-the-Rabbit – not to speak of naughty Rory-the-Nobber, my grandson. This week I want to tell you about Rory's school.

Each morning at this time of year, when there are few horrible hunters about, Rory and his friends trot off to the Tufted-Top-Tree in the Mossieburn, with their schoolbags over their baby horns, where Professor Red-Deer has his morning classes for the boys of the herd. Mrs Red-Deer has another class like her husband's, for the young girls of the herd, but that is much further up the hill. Boys and Girls go to different classes in the Deer Forest, so I can't tell you much about Mrs Red-Deer's classes because I have never been to a girls' class!

Professor Red-Deer is an old, old stag. He has grey hair which is falling out, thin, smooth horns and no teeth because they have been worn away over the years chewing stag grass. He is a dear old boy really (or a real old deer – whichever way you like to put it!) He is very wise and because he is so cunning, the horrible hunters have never – touched him – not even got a shot at him – so he is the best sort of teacher we could have. Rory and six other nobbers are in the class,

*... Lessons start as soon as the sun comes over the Ben More Rock ...*

and they do their best to behave when he is wearing his horns because if they don't, he gets very scratchy and sometimes dishes out horrible whacks with his horns and prods in the ribs with his points. But when he has lost his horns, or when he has tender new ones growing, then the naughty nobbers play up no-how – (even then they risk a bash from the Professor's forefeet).

Lessons start as soon as the sun comes over Ben More Rock, and they finish as it goes down below the horizon at the back of Iona. The nobbers are allowed three ten-munch breaks during the day but have to find their munches in the Mossieburn.

The Old Professor teaches them how to smell, how to spy, how to recognise a horrible hunter.

He teaches them how always to be looking down the hill, with noses to the wind, and how to be sure to have someone in the herd awake at all times.

He teaches them always to walk or run or feed against the wind so that they can smell an enemy as they move.

He teaches them never to stop or look back when they know the enemy are about and to keep on walking as long as they can if they get plugged by a bullet in the bum.

He teaches them how to lie in a peat hag with the dark background of the peat behind their heads, making them hard to see. He teaches them all the danger signals our friends make – the hind's bark, Gorkie's 'Go back, Go back', Olly's 'Twit-a-woo', and the Ptarmigan's 'Coo-Coo'.

In the love-making season, he teaches them how to cover themselves with peat so as to get into a love-making mood.

And then, on Sundays, he puts bracken round his neck, and the nobbers go up to Sunday School – they all kneel in the Mossieburn, with their heads held high and their tails in the air, and pray to the Dear Deer God.

Rory didn't get a very good report last term – he was always ragging about and not listening to the Professor enough. Rory said the old man was too old and could hardly move fast enough to show them what to do, but I told Rory that staggies may get old but, when they do, they get wise as well – and he had better listen to what the old stag says. Poor Rory, he would sooner kick fir cones around than go to Mossieburn School everyday. However, he's only got one more year before he becomes a fully fledged 6-pointer, and then he will probably be a deer-prefect at school and do part-time work with the herd as well.

I think I must close now Henry, as I am going to the Mossieburn to talk to Professor Red-Deer about Rory's future.

I have still got both my horns but they are very sore. Be a good boy, Henry.

Oh! Here comes Golden Eagle Post – I'm just in time.

Your old Pal,

Alby

*… The Professor on Sunday …*

# Letter No. 4 from Alby to Henry

TELEPHONE
STAGLAND 303

SOMEWHERE ON THE ISLE OF MULL
ARGYLL SCOTLAND
14th March

Hello Henry,

... I didn't hear you shout back last week! Did you open the window and shout Hello Alby your loudest? Try again – one, two, three – SHOUT ... I'll let you know next week if I heard you.

I am sorry if last week's letter was a little late. The Golden Eagle Post told me that the wind was against him and that flying over to you was like climbing up your stairs over and over again but never getting to the top!

As you will see from my picture, I have lost one horn – my best horn. It fell off two nights ago with a bang while I was asleep – so I started eating it at once. We always do that as own-horn-meat builds our bodies up stronger than anything. I haven't quite finished it yet. I looked at myself in the burn-pool just now, when I was having breakfast, and I do look rather odd, don't I?

As I told you, I went up to talk to Professor Red Deer about Rory's lessons. He was really very nice about Rory and said he was a clever boy but he doesn't work hard enough. He said Rory's father was the same when at school and has now turned into a lovely young stag – so I mustn't worry. The Professor promised me he would give Rory a bash with his horns and a dig in the ribs with his points every time he yawns next term:

*I started eating my horn at once*

You may not understand, Henry, but in the Deer Forest we don't just have one husband and one wife. We stags collect as many hinds as we can at love-making time in the Autumn. We even fight each other for them. It doesn't matter a hoot what they look like as long as they are hinds!

*Niall is now a beautiful six pointer*

Well, Niall, who is now a beautiful 6-pointer, is one of my many sons, and two years ago in the love-making time he started to fight for hinds himself. Morag was amongst the hinds he won, and Rory was born after that love-making time. He was one of Niall's first sons.

Niall is working for the herd very hard now. He works out where the stags are to eat and sleep and which stag is to be on guard and when. He writes all his instructions in the stag-moss with his hoofs every morning. He has three or four young stags to help him. Every now and again he comes across Rory and his nobber friends doing something they shouldn't be doing, and gives them a ticking off. Sadly, he has just lost both his horns and so he will look rather like a hind for a few months, and he won't like that.

Oh – here come Niall to talk to me. He wants to know if I'll do the midnight smell-watch tonight. I am really too old for this sort of thing but he says two of his regulars have stag-colds and their noses are all blocked up, so I will have to do my little bit. It's a nice night anyway. He also tells me that the herd will be moving up the hill a bit next week as the new green shoots of grass are starting to appear. It is always rather a bother when we move our camp because we have to make new beds in the heather, and they are always cold to start with.

Ronnie, the Roe Deer, such a nice chap, is bounding up the hill. I wonder what he wants – probably had a row with Rory. Oh, no – he wanted to tell me that Golden Eagle Post is filling up his tanks on some old dead rabbits and won't be up this length tonight. Nice Ronnie, he knew I was writing to you today so he has offered to take this letter down to the Myxie rabbit garage where it will be picked up by Golden Eagle Post – so I must finish now. Hope you are being good – I will be without horns altogether next week, I expect – and then I will start to grow my boorful new ones but they won't be tough and ready until after your birthday.

I shall just stamp on this letter and stick it on Ronnie's back with a bit of sello-heather, and he will take it down to the post-birds.

Your ol Pal,

Alby

# Letter No. 5 from Alby to Henry

TELEPHONE
STAGLAND 303

SOMEWHERE ON THE ISLE OF MULL
ARGYLL
SCOTLAND
21st March

Hello Henry,

I couldn't really hear you last time – open the window a little bit more when you get this and shout louder – now ...

I'm a wee bit deaf this morning as my other horn has fallen off, and I feel all light in the head. I wonder what my new ones will be like.

Well, Niall moved us all up the hill last Church-day to a nice little gully about 2,500 feet up Ben More, on the Southern slope, overlooking Loch Scridain. It's very nice up here but a little cold at nights. The green grass shoots are very juicy and taste rather like your French runner beans.

After we had got our new beds made and unpacked our luggage, Professor Red-Deer arrived with heather round his neck, and we had our Church-day Service. We all thanked Dear Deer God for the lovely new bit of hill we had found and asked that we might all turn into booful stags with lovely new big, big horns.

Just as the Service finished, the smell-sentries gave warning of human smells coming nearer. We all got up and sniffed – just in case. Then, about a mile away, to our left, we saw old Hamish, the shepherd, and his collie dog, Trash, climbing the hill to see if the sheep are all well. Hamish's sheep are good friends to us. Like all the others, they give warning when the hunters are about as they run off if the hunters get too close and, as they are white, we can see them for miles.

After we saw that all was clear, we had another munch and lay down again in our new cold beds to try and make them warm.

On the day-after-church-day, me and some of the others went for a walk in the gloaming to see what the grass was like lower down on the west slope of Ben More. It seemed to be growing well. Then we took a stroll over to Chrissie's cottage at Burg. Niall hammered on her window with his tail as his head is too sore. Chrissie came to her door and gave us each a scone which she had been baking. She looked very well and said she hoped to be seeing you and your Daddy and Mummy and Granddaddy and Grandmummy before too long. Then we walked back along the beach of Loch Scridain, past the Tiroran House Hotel and on to have a look at your wee house at Craig. It was dark by the time we got there, but the little house looked well and was longing to see you again. We spent that night in the young trees in front of Craig and came back to the herd in the morning.

I saw Morag and some of the hinds for a moment the other day. She says they are all very well and are spending their time looking for nice little grassy nests where they can each go on their own and have their babies in a few weeks time. She said they were nearly all going to have babies this year, including herself.

It's so much nicer now the snow has finished (I hope!) and the nights are warmer, and as we are out of season, there is little danger. It's at this time we go on expeditions to see what's going on all over the island, and we have long talks with all our friends.

Oh, by the way, the Golden Eagle Postwoman is busy trying to lay an egg so we only have one postman at the moment. As he may fly in a bit over weight and weary, will your dogs, Fred and Olly, leave a little dinner for him. I am sure he would grateful as he uses a lot of myxie petrol when he is carrying all the mail himself, and myxie petrol is rather hard to come by at the moment as most bunnies are down their burrows having babies, like everyone else! Ah – here he comes – his beak does look very full, but I am sure he will manage this one.

Your old friend with no horns,

## Alby

*Trash and Hamish*

# Letter No. 6 from Alby to Henry

TELEPHONE
STAGLAND 303

SOMEWHERE ON THE ISLE OF MULl
ARGYLL
SCOTLAND
28th March

Hello Henry,

I heard you shout very well last weekend, but wasn't it cold?

We had six inches of snow on the top of Ben More. I wondered what was wrong when I woke up because where my horns used to be was freezing cold and then I saw the hills were all white as if it were winter.

Before I had even started to scratch the snow away to get my breakfast, Harry the Hare came lopping along for a gossip. He was all white like the snow. He goes blue when the snow goes and the heather comes – wish we did that, we wouldn't be seen so easily then. Harry said the Freddie Foxes had been very nasty to the hare-family this winter and had eaten many of them. However, he was pleased to hear that Hamish had shot two foxes last week and that Trash, the Collie, had caught one by the tail just as it was going down its hole, where it was going to have babies. We call baby foxes cubs. That is why big Scouts call little Scouts – Cubs.

While we were talking, a big sky monster flew over, miles and miles up in the air, leaving white trails behind it.

14

*… Trash, the collie, had caught one by his tail …*

Harry was interesting about the flying monsters – he said they were flying Jumbos which people got inside. The jumbos put their big ears up, have a meal of spinach and leeks, stick their trunks out in front of them, inhale heaps of fresh air, and stick their tails out behind them. The jets from the spinach and leeks make them fly up high in the sky. Please ask your Dad if this is true and, if so, can I flyaway if I eat spinach and leeks or must I have big ears like the jumbos'.

*… He is so clumsy when he tries to do the horn dance …*

I'm afraid Rory's not doing very well at school this term. His Form-Stag-Master told me he is being very idle at his dancing lessons, so I went down to see him in dancing class. He is so clumsy when he tries to do the horn dance – like your sword dance but done over cast-off horns which haven't been eaten. The trouble is that he keeps on forgetting he has got four legs, and only two have to be used when dancing! However, I think he's trying.

Ah! Here comes the Golden Eagle Postman – heavily laden again – he has got ice on his beak I see. By the way, did those horrible hounds of yours, Fred and Olly, give him some of their dins last week? I do hope so, and I hope they will manage a bit more this week.

Cheerio, Henry

Your old Pal,

Alby

# Letter No. 7 from Alby to Henry

TELEPHONE
STAGLAND 303

SOMEWHERE ON THE ISLE OF MULL
ARGYLL
SCOTLAND
4th April

Hello Henry,

You know, Henry, this is a very quiet time in Stagland. We have all got sore heads because we have new horns just starting, our hair is falling out because new hair is coming, and we have all got sniffly noses because we are very thin and damp. Some of the older stags actually pass away, and those horrible fellows, Roger, the Raven, and Harold the Hoodie, fly about waiting for stag funerals so that they can have a big munch.

Anyway, I suggested to Niall that we had a full-scale practice for 'hunting time' so that we are all ready when the horrible hunters come. He agreed, and we were all told to go to the high tops on the day after church-day. There we lay as if we were in 'hunting time' – smell-sentries all round, little parties of nobbers a little way off with me in the middle. Rory thought this was stupid as we didn't look like us with no horns on – so he and a friend of his lay on their backs, behind a rock, with their forefeet crossed and their back legs crossed – all sticking up over the rock to look like horns. Brown Bunny and Harry the Hare, who came with us, tried to make their big ears look like horns too, but they weren't very good.

When we were all ready, one of the smell-sentries suddenly got up and sniffed, and then another and then some of the stags in the middle of the herd and then me and then everyone (only pretending of course). Then Niall led off down the hill at the gallop with us all following – but Bunny and Harry couldn't keep up however much they tried. Down the hill we went, right to the burn, and then up the other side, where we stopped and sniffed – just like what we do if it was real. Then I noticed how everyone was panting and puffing, so I told Niall he would have to

17

make all of us much fitter before the horrible hunters arrived.

The following day, Niall took the whole herd jogging. He told us we must all be in step – left front, left back, right front, right back – slowly trot – one – two – three – four, and at the same time, singing the 'Jogging Song'.

> One Two, One Two,
> All Stags move, not-just-a-few.
> Knees up, Knees up,
> Old or young – never give up.
> Jog along, Jog along,
> As you sing this happy song.
> Left up, Right up,
> Back and Front,
> Head up, Tail up,
> Smile and Grunt, Smile and Grunt.

After we had jogged once around the top of the Ben, Ronnie, the Roe came out of the wood laughing with big grunts (his new horns are nearly dear of velvet). Niall told him to stop laughing or go way – or, said Niall, 'Whistle a tune' – so Ronnie stood on a rock and whistled the 'Jogging Song', and we jogged, and we jogged, and we jogged. Why don't you try jogging, Henry – do it for an hour at dawn each morning, and then we'll know that we're all doing it together.

I meant to tell you, Henry, that last Church-day we all took fir tree branches 'in our mouths and laid them on the ground, one behind the other in memory of Fir-Tree-Church-day a long time ago, when Little-Lord-Jesus-Stag entered the Mossieburn only four days before he was murdered. Little-Lord-Jesus-Stag was a very, very wonderful stag who still watches over us and loves us all. Each year we remember his last days on Ben More with a special Church-day service in the Mossieburn, when everybody comes, even Roger the Raven and the Golden-Eagle-Post. That happens next Church-day. I will tell you all about it in my next letter.

Here come Roger – I wonder what he wants – oh, it's the same problem as last week. Golden-Eagle-Post can't get up here so Roger is going to take this to him at the Myxie Garage – hope he doesn't eat it on the way – he eats most things – dirty old bird.

Be a good boy, Henry – my new horns are coming on fine – they may even be showing by next week.

Your old friend,

Alby

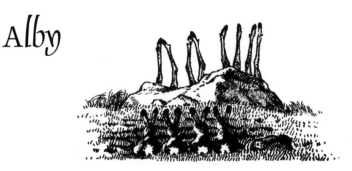

*… Rory and a friend lay on their backs behind a rock with their legs crossed …*

*Stag Easter Day*

# Letter No. 8 from Alby to Henry

TELEPHONE
STAGLAND 303

SOMEWHERE ON THE ISLE OF MULL
ARGYLL
SCOTLAND
11th April

Hello Henry,

Thank you for calling so loud last week – it was lovely to hear you as we all jogged round the Ben. Have you been jogging, Henry?

By the way, do you see my horns have started to grow – just a teeny weeny bit, but they are very soft and hurt if I bang them on anything.

I hope you had a happy Stag-Easter like what we did and that you went to a lovely Church-day Service.

Our one was wonderful- all dear-deer-God's people were there. They started coming in at dawn from all Stagland to join together at the Mossieburn. It was a beautiful clear morning, with blue skies and the odd flying Jumbo crossing with its white smoke trails. There was little wind and, if you kept quiet, you could just hear the cars and buses going past Craignure. There was a big tanker and several sailing boats in the Sound of Mull and some more boats lying at anchor near Iona. The sea was very calm.

I got up, scratched my hair, made my bed and had a little new-grass-breakfast with the other stags – they were all licked-polished and looking so very happy. Then, round the corner of the Ben came the hinds, led by old Morag – all looking very booful but a little slow on their feet as most of them are going to have babies soon. Then Brown Bunny, his wife and Mr and Mrs Harry Hare came, walking slowly along over the burnt heather – all looking so smart with their furry coats boofully brushed. Gorkie the cock grouse came in with a Miss Partridge, 'cos he can't find another grouse wife. Mr and Mrs Freddie Fox came along behind them – but Freddie knew that this was no day for biting people's heads off, however tempting they looked. Olly the owl and

*... all the birds found branches to sit on ...*

20

*… Professor and Mrs Red Deer arrive for the service with heather round their necks …*

Golden-Eagle-Post with Roger the Raven and Harold the Hoodie all glided in very silently and found birch branches to sit on. Then our group went down, all smart in our jogging formation, singing our 'Jogging Song'.

It really was a lovely sight, Henry, all dear-deer-God's family sitting, standing and perching together around the big stone at the edge of the birch wood by the Mossieburn. Rory came and sat beside me. He was looking very smart and behaved really, really well all day. I looked back, at one moment, and saw Mr MacTavish and Hamish the Shepherd and Trash the Collie all sitting on a mound well up the hill and watching us through their binoculars. They would like to be with us because you see, Henry, although they are like you, not me, we are all part of dear-deer-God's family – even the switches who were amongst us (but, of course, we couldn't tell who the switches were because they had no horns. Dear-deer-God knew them all right ! In case you don't know, Henry, switches are nasty stags that just have big long spikes on their head rather than points like proper stags!).

Then, as the sun came over the Ben, it was time to start the Service. Olly hooted, Ronnie whistled, Gorkie chuckled, Freddie barked, Roger and Harry the Hoodie crowed, and all the Red Deer stood up on their hind legs and clapped with their front paws. Away in the distance we heard Trash say 'Wuff-Wuff'. I believe, before the Service starts, you ring bells to call people to church.

Then through the trees came Professor and Mrs Red Deer, with heather round their necks, followed by two Foxes, two Roe Deer, two Brown Bunnies, two White Hares, and sitting on their backs were two Ravens, two Hoodies and two Owls. They walked very solemnly to the big stone

21

and arranged themselves round it. There wasn't a sound except for the trickle of the Mossieburn down in the wood. All the birds got off the backs of the animals and found branches or pieces of heather to sit on.

Then the Professor welcomed us and asked us to sing a Stagland song, saying 'thank you' to dear-deer-God for all the people that were together and for the lovely things they could all see. The birds tweeted and the animals grunted so the noise that came out was a sort of twee-grunt (wonder if you can make a twee-grunt, Henry?) And so we all tweegrunted as loudly as we could:

> Stag-Jesus we do love Thee,
> We love Thee very much,
> Please tell your deer-God Daddie
> His coat we long to touch.

And there were many more verses like that one. And then the Professor asked us to kneel and pray. You remember I told you how we did that, Henry – we knelt down on our forelegs, keeping our head up and our tail up. We all wag our tails at the end of each prayer – I believe you say 'Amen'.

Then the Professor told us all the story of Stag-Jesus.

'It was hundreds and hundreds of years ago when a stag, who mended other stags' horns, helped a hind to have a calf in a bog because all the other deer were lying on the only bit of heather on the hill. You see, it was Winter', he said, 'and there wasn't very much dry ground to lie on, especially as it was at a time when all stags had been called together to discuss where they were going to get their Winter grazing from.

'Well, the calf, who was called Stag-Jesus, grew into a very ordinary looking six-pointer, but he was very special in other ways. He could mend stags' wounds if they were shot by the horrible hunters. He could make the silly old hinds happy when they got nasty smell-coughs. He said he was the son of dear-deer-God, and he gave hundreds of talks to the people of Stagland, helping them, telling them off, healing them, and, as time went on, he found more and more friends. But he had no friends amongst the nasty cruel switches who thought they ruled Stagland because of the sharp points they had on their horns. They became real enemies of Stag-Jesus. They did not believe he was the son of dear-deer-God and, in case he became more powerful than them, they decided to murder him. Stag-Jesus knew this and asked his Daddie, dear-deer-God, if he could help him, but his Daddie told him he had to go through with whatever happened next, and if he was murdered, he had got to prove that good cannot be killed, only evil – so that was the way it was to be.

'One cold night, a party of switches went to the top of Ben More to murder Stag-Jesus. They knew he was there with some of his friends but, when they found them, the switches didn't know which one was Stag-Jesus. Then one of his friends

betrayed him by licking the brow point of Stag-Jesus' horns. You see, Henry, this nasty friend had been given money by the switches to give Stag-Jesus away – a very nasty thing to do.  .

'The switches quickly chased Stag-Jesus from the small herd. They chased him up the hill to the top, where they stood round him until dawn. Then they pushed Stag-Jesus against a rock and charged him with their sharp switch horns – stabbing him over and over again. One after the other they charged him, but there was nothing Stag-Jesus could do except cry out as it hurt so much. Then he passed out and they licked his wounds until he became conscious again. Then they started to dig their switch horns into him once more, and eventually he died in terrible pain.

'Stag-Jesus had a great friend called Jo, who saw all this happening, and after Stag-Jesus had died, Jo went to the switches and asked if he could move Stag-Jesus' body to a cave down on the shores of Loch-na-Keal. The switches couldn't care less – Stag-Jesus was dead, so what could it matter.

'Jo and some friends made a stretcher from the fir branches used last Church-day and put Stag-Jesus on to it. Then they carried him between their horns to the cave on the beach, and they laid him in it. Then Jo and his friends managed to push a huge stone that looked like an egg over the front of the cave and left him there. That was two days before Church-day.

'On the day after Church-day, some of the hinds wanted to go and put some lovely white flowers from the stag-moss at the mouth of the cave, but when they got there they found the egg-like stone had been rolled away, and there was no sign of Stag-Jesus. They were very frightened and blamed the horrible switches for taking the body away.

'So all the hinds who were there went in search – some one way, some another.

Suddenly a party of three old hinds saw a stag pulling at the coarse grass beside the sands along the bay. When they got near the stag, they saw his coat was covered in blood, and there were holes in his body. It was Stag-Jesus – alive and well. He looked up, chewing the cud, and smiled at them, and told them to go and tell his chums he was OK and would like to see them on the beach. Within an hour all the good people of Stagland, together with some people of the sea whales, sharks, porpoises, fish, lobsters, crabs and others – were on the beach, listening to Stag-Jesus' stories and instructions. They listened to him for a long, long time.

'And then, one day, a few weeks later, they followed him up Ben More, and he told them always to love his Daddie-in-Heaven, never to hate the switch-stags because they didn't know what they were doing when they killed him, and always to love one another and all of his Daddie's creatures, even Freddie and Harry and Roger. While he was talking, they got to the top of the Ben, but Stag-Jesus went on walking – up and up and up – 'til he got lost amongst the clouds where the flying jumbos live. As his voice died away, they could hear him saying he would always look after them and asking them always to be good people and to talk to him through prayer as often as possible – then, in a sort of whisper that everyone heard, he said "I'll be back one day" – and he was gone.'

And that was the end of the Professor's story. We all felt very humble, and as the Professor, his wife and his twee-grunters went away through the birch trees, so everyone else went back to their homes in Stagland. As we went, we all twee-grunted that lovely song – 'Now thank we all Stag-Jesus'.

I'm sorry, Henry, that it is such a long letter this week, but Stag-Easter is a great day in Stagland, and I am sure it is in your land too. Ask Dad or Mum to read you your story of Little Lord Jesus at Easter-time. You'll find it's very like ours.

And, Henry, every time you get an Easter egg or open one and find a present, remember that great big egg shaped stone that was rolled across the cave. It hid the greatest present this world had ever known.

Now it must be time for you to go to sleep. All your very special friends in Stagland send their love to you and your Mum and Dad and Fred and Olly at this very special time. In fact, they send their love to everyone – even the switch stags. Sleep well, Henry, and say 'thank-you' – not to me – but to your own little Lord Jesus, before you turn over and shut your eyes.

# Alby

# Letter No. 9 from Alby to Henry

TELEPHONE
STAGLAND 303

SOMEWHERE IN THE ISLE OF MULL
ARGYLL
SCOTLAND
18th April

Helloo Henry,

I heard you beautifully last week – sound travels so slowly that your 'HELLO' arrived at the top of Ben More just as the Golden-Eagle-Post returned!

Henry – bad news this week. Rory has been in real trouble. In fact he was sent to Professor Red Deer to be punished along with those two naughty nobber neighbours who belong to the stag herd above Bunessan. They are always leading him astray. Now they have all been put in the corner at the bottom of the Glen for two days, with 'WE ARE NAUGHTY NOBBERS' written in stag moss on their backsides.

This is what happened:

Two days after Church-day last week, I had just got out of bed and was enjoying my early morning lick of dew when I noticed the two naughty nobber neighbours lying beside Rory, quite close to Rory's Dad, Niall, who was on smell-sentry as usual. I knew Rory would wake up before long because there was a huge bluebottle fly which kept on flying in one of his ears and out the other, making a horrid buzzing noise. Then it suddenly flew up his nose and came out of his mouth and settled on one of his new soft nobs. Rory woke up in a bait and tried to find the fly to swat it but couldn't see it as it was perching just above his eyes on the nob. The two naughties woke up as well and were hooting with laughter at Rory's problem.

Rory went to Niall, his Dad, and said he couldn't stand the flies any more and would it be all right if he and the naughties went off for a stroll down the hill. Niall agreed on condition they were back in time for tea-moss as the sun went down.

Off went Rory and the two naughties down the hill at the gallop, playing leapfrog as they went. Every now and again, a naughty would slip on a stone and bash his new nobs against it – grunting in agony as he did so.

Well, the three nobbers went on down the hill, larking about as they went, until they got to the Loch-side where they played 'hide-and-seek' in the sand dunes – then they climbed back up the hill to have a scrummy mossy lunch in the Treetop bog. It had been a lovely day but, while they were eating, it seemed to get darker – and darker – and darker until they suddenly realised that they were enveloped in mist. Rory got into a panic and said they must hurry back up the hill, but the naughties said 'No, no, let's finish our scrummy lunch and smell our way back against the wind after we have had a zizz', and played some more 'hide-and-seek'. They did have a zizz, and they did play more 'hide and-seek', and they did start off home against the wind – but, Henry, the wind HAD CHANGED! They weren't going UP the hill, they were going DOWN the hill, and it was getting a much blacker kind of dark than it had been. They started to get frightened in case they got lost, but their fear was taken away by the lovely smell of lusher and lusher grass. They walked very slowly and carefully, longing to get to that sweet-smelling grass.

*… Jumped off the ants' nest onto the others back …*

Suddenly they came to a huge high fence but the lush smelling grass was on the other side if it. They were walking up and down the fence, trying to find a hole, when one of the naughties noticed a big ants' nest about forty yards back from the fence. He suggested they should go back behind it, gallop to the top of it, take a big leap and, hopefully, would clear the top of the fence and find the lush smelling grass. They all tried this many times but never got over. They hurt their nobs, bruised their knees, bust their toes, but never got over.

Then the other naughty suggested they played sort of double leapfrog with the ants' nest. He would stand between it and the fence and the others would jump from the ants' nest on to his back and, with one more spring, would be over the fence. They tried it one naughty acting as a jumping place while the other came rushing down the hill, jumped off the ants' nest, on to the other naughty's back, who gave a little kick while he jumped off again and so over the fence, landing ten feet below on his nose in a bog of 'oh, such booful grass'. Then Rory did the same thing and landed the same way – on his nose in the bog in the booful grass. That left one naughty the wrong side of the fence all by himself. He tried many times to jump it on his own but he always fell backwards, and in the end was so sore from falling that he just stayed where he was and hoped that his chums would push some of the new found beautiful grass through the wire to him – which they did.

Meanwhile, Rory and the first naughty walked on, getting into the lusher grass as they went – some good yellow flowers too and lovely bushes. Eventually they had eaten so much that they lay down in a booful blooming heather bed, next to a small pond, with big stone statues all round them and went to sleep. The naughty outside the fence went to sleep as well.

*... A naval cannon pointing at them outside of the window ...*

In the morning they woke up to a clear day – the mist had gone and, oh, Henry, oh dear, they were in the middle of the Gardens of Torosay Castle, and had eaten all the lovely azaleas and many of the roses and, oh, horror – there at the top window of the castle was the castle caretaker in his night-shirt and night-cap, with a naval cannon pointing at them out of the window. There was a lighted match in his hand and he was all ready to send the cannon ball straight at them at hundreds of miles an hour. He was saying horrible things too, Henry.

Rory picked a white coloured daffodil in his mouth and waved it furiously in surrender but, as he did so, he noticed the castle gardener, coming out of the castle garden door, with a double-barrelled shotgun under his arm, a steel helmet on his head and a sword buckled round his pyjamas.

Meanwhile, the naughty outside the fence had woken up and seen the horrible plight his chums were in:

'Come back, come back', he grunted.

'We can't get back', retorted Rory.

'Well, charge them, or they'll make you into sausages', grunted the naughty.

Oh dear, here comes Golden Eagle Post. I must give him this but will continue the sad story of Torosay Gardens in my next.

Cheerio, Henry, be a good boy.

Rory hates looking at the bank in the corner of the glen.

# Alby

*Rory waves a white daffodil in surrender*

# Letter No. 10 *from Alby to Henry*

TELEPHONE
STAGLAND 303

SOMEWHERE ON THE ISLE OF MULL
ARGYLL
SCOTLAND
25th April

Hello Henry,

Isn't it lovely that the weather is getting warmer and my horns are starting to grow a bit. Rory has come out of his corner-in-the-glen, feeling very sorry for himself for the trouble he caused at Torosay through not doing what his Daddy told him. He's longing for rain to wash the 'Naughty-nobber' notice off his backside.

However, I must go on with the sad story of the Torosay Gardens. You will remember I told you in my last letter that the nobber outside the fence had grunted to his friend and Rory to charge the castle gardener and escape. Well, Henry, they had put their heads down to charge, the nobber outside the fence was already cheering; but just as they were about to charge, there was a loud 'bang'. They looked up and saw the cannon on the top floor of the castle hurtling out of the window. The castle caretaker was hanging on to the back of it, with his night-shirt trailing behind him. The ball had stuck and wouldn't come out of the barrel, so the whole gun took off when the powder exploded, and the castle caretaker forgot to let go. It came on and on. It flew so low over the castle gardener that the draught knocked the gun out of his hand and he fell to the ground. On it went and eventually landed on the new bridge in the Japanese Garden, breaking it in two and pulling the castle caretaker into the mud of the Japanese pond behind it. When he got up, he

*… And the caretaker forgot to let go …*

was talking naughty-naughty language, and he looked like a great big black crow. All three nobbers hooted with laughter, and the two in the garden trotted up the garden terraces and in through the garden door of the castle, where they smelt buns, but:

As they went past the room with the telephone in it, they overheard the castle gardener's lady on the telephone to Constable Donald at Craignure – she was telling him to come quickly as there were two four-legged robbers in the garden. She told him to bring his gun, to ring up the soldiers' camp at Tobermory and arrange for helicopter cover everything must happen at once – it was urgent. At that moment, she saw two nobbers looking through the door and threw the telephone at them, but it didn't get very far because the wire was firmly fastened to the wall.

The nobbers took fright and ran out of the front of the house, across the grass and into the nearest rhododendron bush. After a moment they heard a strange noise ahead of them, like a car trying to start. They crept forward and, do you know what, Henry? They saw an old man trying to start the engine on the model Torosay railway. Rory had a bright idea. He smiled at the old man and suggested that he and his friend might pull the train by the towrope until the engine started. This was agreed. The two nobbers were harnessed by the towrope and started to pull the engine with its three coaches attached. Chug – chug – chug it went in a slow sad way as they moved slowly down the line.

'Hurry up', said the old man, 'I must be at Craignure in time to meet the passengers off the Oban boat and take them to the castle.'

The nobbers tried harder and quite suddenly the Chug – chug – chug turned into a

Chugchugchug, and a puff of smoke came out of the funnel. The engine was going. The old man untied the towrope. Rory jumped into one carriage and his friend into another, and the train went off full blast down the hill through the woods.

As the train rushed down the hill at thirty miles an hour, it passed Constable Donald, on the main road, bicycling up the hill towards the Castle, with his gun over his shoulder, his Alsatian at his back wheel and a fierce look on his face. He turned to wave to the old train driver and, as he did so, he thought he saw the nobbers on the train but he wasn't sure, he wasn't sure, he wasn't sure – should he bicycle on towards the Castle or turn round and chase the train? He decided to go on to the Castle as requested, and he could always telephone his wife at Craignure and ask her to see if the nobbers really were on the train.

Rory was worried about what to do when the train stopped. He was even more worried when he saw overhead the Golden Eagle Post, Roger the Raven, Harold the Hoodie, Olly the Owl, Gorkie the Grouse and his partridge girlfriend, and all the other birds from Stagland, flying round in circles with twigs sticking out of their beaks.

You see, Henry, when the nobbers never came back the night before, Niall had raised the alarm and asked all flying friends to get airborne in the morning and see what they could find out, while all smell-sentries did a land search. The twigs in the birds' mouths were sort of wireless aerials and whenever a bird saw something of interest he would waggle his twig. Then all the birds would. waggle their twigs, and the smell-sentries would see the twigs waggling. Then they would know there was something to look at on the ground under the birds.

The train raced on as the old man hooted its hooter to tell all the people that the train was on its way. Rory knew that when it reached Craignure, ALL the horrible humans would be out for their blood. There was only one answer – they had to escape by water.

I must stop there for this week, Henry, as Freddie the Fox has just called to say that Golden Eagle Post is so busy catching Brown Bunnies and things to put in Mrs Golden Eagle's nest, for her to feed her babies on when the eggs hatch, that he cannot come up for the mail. However Freddie is going down to Myxie Garage with it for me. I'll finish the story of the Castle Gardens next week. Now I must go and see that Rory is doing his homework because his Dad, Niall, is off duty tonight as he wanted to go to a social in the Mossieburn School.

Goodnight Henry,

Alby

# Letter No. 11 *from Alby to Henry*

TELEPHONE
STAGLAND 303

SOMEWHERE ON THE ISLE OF MULL
ARGYLL
SCOTLAND
2nd May

Hello Henry,

Hello! Hello! Hello!

I must try and finish the Torosay Story this week as otherwise we'll get very behind with the news from up here.

You remember last week the Post came just as I was telling you about Rory and his chums going full speed downhill in the model train, with the old man hooting the hooter in front. The old man was trying to get to Craignure in time to pick up the tourists off the ferry and take them to Torosay Castle.

Well, as they were nearing the landing place, where there were a lot of people, Rory saw an old Land Rover coming down the road going three times as fast as the train and passing it. It was being driven by the castle gardener in his night-cap, and sitting on the top was the castle caretaker with his cannon – still covered in mud. Then Rory saw that some of the people waiting had guns which they were loading, while overhead the birds from Stagland circled sending messages back to Ben More by twig radio. When the train stopped, they would have to move fast. It stopped with an ugly screech and a puff of smoke.

Rory and his friend jumped off the train, ran through the crowd – no one could shoot in case they shot each other – on to the deck of the ferry, up the ladder, through the main cabin, past the bridge, down the ladder, and a last fast run to the front of the boat.

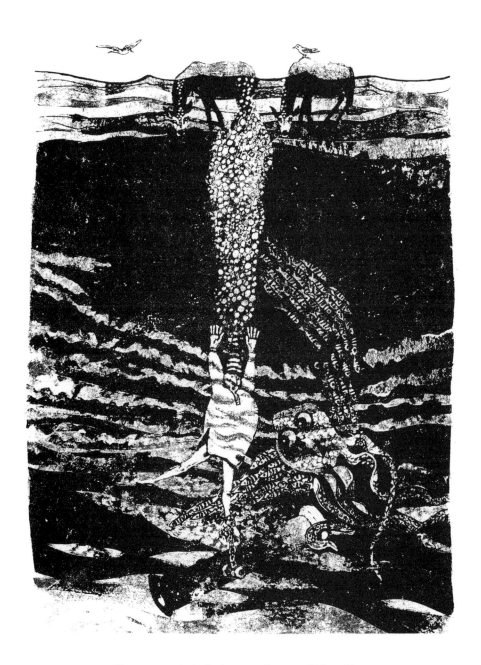

*… The cannon chain had got stuck around his ankle …*

Then they jumped out – out – out – out into the Sound of Mull. Down – down – down they went, and then a splash, and then further down until they thought they were going to drown – ooh, it was cold for them. At last they came up spluttering and splashing.

They had only just had time to clear their eyes and have a look around when there was a big splash just ahead. It was the castle caretaker with his cannon and all. The same thing had happened again! He had fired the cannon from his Land Rover. The cannon ball had got stuck, and the explosion had carried him, and his cannon, over the ferry and way out to where they had jumped, but this time the castle caretaker was in trouble. The cannon chain had got stuck round his ankle, and the cannon was pulling him down. He shouted to the nobbers for help. Naughty swam up to him and put him on his back while Rory held the cannon to take the weight off. The Caretaker was in a terrible state, and asked to be taken ashore.

'Only if you promise you will get us back to Stagland without hurt,' said Naughty. 'OK – OK,' said the Caretaker, 'but we had better swim up to Fishnish where there will be fewer people.'

Anyway, thought Rory, they won't shoot at us with the Caretaker on Naughty's back – so they undid the cannon and let it sink to the bottom of the sea, and made the Caretaker secure on the back of Naughty and started swimming west.

Then, Henry, the poor nobbers saw terrible things happen. First two gun boats could he seen speeding towards them from Craignure, then an electric canoe with two policemen, headed across the Sound from Morven, then a destroyer came out of Loch Sunart, then, worst of all, 22

helicopters in line ahead came from the direction of Oban. One of the pilots had a stink bomb, which he dropped – and that was the signal for the other 21 helicopters to release their stink bombs. They exploded when they hit the water, making such a horrid, horrid smell that the destroyer and the gunboats and the Police canoe all thought they were being gassed so went into reverse. They stayed that way until they had disappeared, while the helicopters flew above the nobbers cheering them on.

Well, Henry they swam for an hour and a half before they reached Fishnish, and every now and again the caretaker changed from one nobber's back to the other.

They got to the pier with no trouble and the caretaker told them to hide under it while he went to find a safe way of getting ashore. There were quite a lot of people about although they had expected to find no one.

The Caretaker said he would whistle when it was safe for them to come ashore. So, after the nobbers had got under the pier, the Caretaker swam off on his own and clambered up the sands. Amongst the crowd there were soldiers and policemen and horrible hunters and fierce looking dogs and many, many guns. The birds from Stagland were still overhead, sending messages of worry back to Ben More.

The Caretaker called for the crowd to come round him – they did. He then spoke to them.

'Friends,' he said, 'I have just been saved from drowning by two brave nobbers. I have promised to see them safely back to Stagland. They may have ruined Torosay Gardens but please give them a hero's welcome.' Then he blew his whistle, and the two nobbers swam slowly round the pier to the shore and walked up the beach, shaking the water off as they went, and very frightened in case they should suddenly become sausages.

As they approached, the crowd formed a lane. The soldiers in front with their rifles at the 'Present' and the rest behind.

The procession moved up the road, through the lane made by the people. Led by a piper, followed by the drummers, then the caretaker with the two nobbers. Everyone else came along behind. When they all got to the gate through the high fence into Stagland, they found it open, and standing beside it, the castle gardener 'at the salute'. Beside him was the naughty nobber who had been left outside the fence and who now joined his two chums. The castle caretaker joined the castle gardener, the Pipes and Drums stood opposite, and the three nobbers marched through the gates on their hind legs, with their heads and eyes facing right in salute to the Castle Gardener and the Castle Caretaker. The gate was then closed. The nobbers got back on all fours and started up the hill. The pipes played *Rory's Return to Ben More* and faded into the distance as the piper marched back to his car.

*... And the three nobbers marched through the gates on their hind legs ...*

The three nobbers were chatting hard about everything that had happened. But when they rounded the first corner, they met two huge stag policemen. 'You are under arrest,'

said the largest, 'we have to take you to Professor Red Deer's Court in Mossieburn.'

'Oh dear,' the nobbers thought, 'and after all that.'

'What have we done?' Rory asked.

'You are charged first with not obeying your Daddie, Stag Niall, and, secondly, with

"getting a bad name for Stagland" by making a mess of Torosay Gardens.'

Half an hour later they arrived at Mossieburn Court. The Professor was standing on a tree trunk, looking very severe. The three nobbers stood sadly in front of him.

He told them they may have been brave boys but they had not obeyed Rory's Dad, Niall. They had caused great offence to the castle gardener. They had caused the castle caretaker to loose his cannon. They had caused much trouble to the Soldiers, the Police, the people of Mull, and all the Stagland Birds; therefore, if they had nothing to say – and they hadn't – they would spend three days standing in the corner of the glen with 'Naughty Nobber' notices stuck on their backsides. All three nobbers said they were sorry and that they would never, never be naughty again. The Professor trotted off, and the two police stags led them to the corner of the glen and put the notices on their backsides with stagmoss. The nobbers were very, very sorry.

Well, that's all that happened, Henry – the nobbers are OK now but they had a nasty three days.

Here's poor wee Rory coming to see me – he knows I am writing today, and he said he would post the letter for me. He sends you his best wishes and says he feels very ashamed.

Grunt, Grunt.

Alby

*This is a stagshot of our Monarch taken last year when he was looking his best*

# Letter No. 12 from Alby to Henry

TELEPHONE
STAGLAND 303

SOMEWHERE ON THE ISLE OF MULL
ARGYLL
SCOTLAND
9th May

Cuckoo, Henry –

Have you got some cuckoos down at Fossoway. There are dozens up here and they 'cuckoo' all day long – a lovely sound but they are nasty birds, Henry, because they go and pinch other people's nests and hatch out other people's eggs – that's why there are so many cuck-pigeons and oo-sparrows flying about.

Anyway, next week we elect our Stag Parliament. That means we all vote for the stag in our herd we want to look after us. The five that get most votes form our council. Then our Council joins the councils from the other herds, and together they form a Parliament. It is Parliament who guards us, leads us and tells us where to get our meals and makes our laws. As you know, Rory's Dad, Niall, has been the Chairman of our Council all this past year, and a very good one too, so I shall vote for him again – I'll tell you how the Election goes in my next.

Our real 'head' is the 'Monarch of the Glen', and I thought I would tell you a bit about him this week. He's a huge big, big stag, Henry, with 12 points on his head – great big points – and weighs 22 stone 7 lbs. At love-making time in October, he roars so loudly that the earth quakes for a mile around him, and this makes his 122 wives very proud of him. He lives on a private pinnacle over on Laggan Forest with a very powerful smell-sentry guard because many horrible hunters would give thousands of pounds to have his big, big head hanging over their loo!

A week or two before love-making time, he roams the island with his bodyguard and visits all the stag herds first and all the hind herds afterwards (that's when he chooses his 122 wives but they are usually the same ones as last year). When he comes to our herd, we all get up and bend our front knees so that our noses are touching the ground, but we mustn't be too close when we do it otherwise our horns might get him on the neb, and then he would bring his big, big horns crashing down on our snouts! He always brings some help-stags with him, who run messages and tell us what to grunt back if he grunts to us, and what sort of grass to offer him at Mossie lunch-time, etc.

Last year when he visited, we did not have much warning, and Rory was playing blind man's buff with some of his nobber friends. When the friends saw 'The Monarch' they fled in fear, leaving Rory trying to find them with his blindfold on. Needles to say, Rory 'Found' 'The Monarch' and pinched his bottom to prove it, saying:

'Found you, Found you,

Teehee hee, Teehee hee

I'll put my hoofs around you, round you.'

'The Monarch' gave such a big grunt, that it blew Rory's blindfold off, and when he saw who he had pinched, all the hair fell off the top of his head, and he went down on his knees, with his head buried in a wet peaty hole so that he couldn't hear what 'The Monarch' said, and that was just as well!

Later on, 'The Monarch' had staggiemoss lunch with us, and was very nice to Rory, and Rory behaved very well. So well, in fact, that 'The Monarch' asked Rory to be his page at the Opening of Stag Parliament this year. (That is the week after next). Rory was so thrilled that he asked if he could go and start polishing his hairs straight away. 'The Monarch' said 'Yes', and Rory vanished down towards the Mossieburn to start getting polished up.

Just before sundown, 'The Monarch' and his helpers left our home and started down the Mossieburn track for Bunessan, where he was due next morning. He grunted many words of encouragement before leaving, said he hoped we would enjoy the Opening of

Stag Parliament and that he hoped we would not suffer too much from the horrible hunters when they started chasing us in a month or two's time. As he walked off, the sun was setting over Iona. He had smell-guards all round him and we could see what a really magnificent stag he was.

Next week I'll tell you how the Election went.

Here's the post. Golden Eagle Post's eggs are bursting to burst!

Be a good boy, Henry

Alby

Henry –
Twig Radio
are resting on
my horns!

# Letter No. 13 from Alby to Henry

TELEPHONE
STAGLAND 303

SOMEWHERE ON THE ISLE OF MULL
ARGYLL
SCOTLAND
16th May

Henry, Henry, HENRY,

Are you OK? I forgot to mention last week that I never heard you shouting 'HELLO ALBEE' when you were staying at Craig the week before. I had given my letter to your woofer Fred, to deliver, as Ronnie the Roe found him chasing Brown Bunnies over the boulders and told him I had a letter to deliver. He had come to see us on Ben More to tell us that his stupid pal, your Olly, was being stupider than ever, and had been sent back to school. Anyway he took my letter and bounded off down the hill. I hope he didn't eat it on the way – if he did, let me know by Golden Eagle Post, and I'll send you a stagshot copy next week.

Well, Henry, this week was election week, when the stag herds elected their Councils. Our herd jogged down to Mossieburn where we found two stags waiting for us at the edge of the trees. One was a booful old stag (rather like the Police Stags). He told us that we must vote for Niall, because Niall was a really steady fellow who cared for other stags and wanted to help them in every way he could. He said that Niall believed that all stags should be allowed to do what they wanted with their stag-lives, and no stag should have to pay bigger moss-taxes than others even if he had more moss than others.

The other stag that met us was a nasty little switch who said we must vote for his switch-friend

*… Made a scratch on one of the trees …*

because he would tax most all the stags who had found a lot of moss – so that the others, who hadn't found much, could be the same as those who had.

He had a mass of red bog myrtle round his neck which was not nearly so pretty as Niall's 'bluebells of Scotland'.

Anyway, we all went behind a big bush one by one so that no one could see us, and made a scratch on one of two trees – either the one behind Niall, in which case we voted for Niall, or the one behind the switch, in which case we voted for the switch.

When the whole herd had made their marks Professor Red Deer arrived and grunted that the voting was finished and now the tellers would have to count the marks on each tree – a very important job. He called on Rory and another nobber, who was very scruffy, to come and count. The scruffy one had to count Niall's votes and Rory the switch's. You see, Henry, it might have looked unfair if Rory counted his Daddie's votes.

We all sat down and waited.

After a short twee-grunt song by his church followers, the Professor called for Niall and the switch candidate and Rory and the switch who was counting Niall's votes to come forward and stand behind him. Then the Professor faced the herd and grunted very loudly:

'Switch-Teller – how many votes have you got?'

Rory stuttered a bit with fright because he is a very bad adder and then grunted – 'Thirty-two Sir – I mean, sorry Sir, twenty-three.'

'WHICH', roared the Professor.

'Twenty-three', grunted Rory.

Then the Professor turned to the young switch

'Stag-teller – how many votes have you got?'

'Seventy-six, Sir', grunted the switch-teller.

Then the Professor put some peat on his face, raised his right foreleg and proclaimed: 'I, Professor Red Deer, the Returning Stag for the parish of Mossieburn, declare that Stag-Niall has been duly elected member of Council for this parish' ... he thought for a moment what 23 was from 76, when Rory grunted out:

'By Fifty-three votes, Sir.' You see Henry, Rory is very good at multiplying and dividing – he is also very good at subtracting – but he is bad at adding.

All that stags clapped with their forelegs except for a few at the back who made nasty grunts. Then Niall came forward and shook the switch by the foreleg. He told the herd that he promised to look after them this year just as well as he did last year. He thanked the Professor for all he had done and thanked that stupid little switch-teller for counting his votes so well.

Then many of the herd came and congratulated Niall. I was very proud of him and told him so. You see, Henry to have a son member of the herd Council makes an old stag like me feel very happy.

The whole herd jogged back to the top of the Ben, very grateful to dear-deer-God that Niall was their member again, and Rory went off to think of all the things he had to do before the Opening of Parliament next week, when he would be page to 'The Monarch'.

All through the day, the birds of Stagland had been floating overhead with twigs in their mouths, sending twig messages to all their friends, telling them how the voting was going, because, Henry, this was a very important day in Stagland.

Judging by the twig-messages we got, the elections at the other herds went very well too – so we should have a good Parliament this year.

Very easy to post this one, Henry, as old Golden Eagle Post is floating just above me.

I'll wave a twig. Here he comes, swooping down. He says his wife's eggs still haven't cracked.

Think of Rory next week, Henry when he is page to 'The Monarch' at the Opening of Parliament – it will be a great day for him.

Your Old Chum

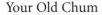

Alby

*… To look at themselves in still water …*

# Letter No. 14 from Alby to Henry

TELEPHONE
STAGLAND 303

SOMEWHERE ON THE ISLE OF MULL
ARGYLL
SCOTLAND
23rd May

Hello Henry,

I am so hoarse after all the twee-grunting after the Opening of Stag Parliament that I can hardly shout to you. However, before I tell you about that wonderful day, I have some very big, big news.

Each year on the day before Stag Parliament opens, all the stags in the herd go down to the Mossie Burn pool in the birch wood to look at themselves in the still water and see if they have any horn awards – that is whether or not they have more points than last year. Although our new horns are still covered in velvet, we can just make out how many points we are going to have.

Well Henry, Rory's so excited, he's going to be a baby six-pointer. His Dad, Niall's going to be a ten-pointer, and Henry, Oh Henry, I'm going to be a ROYAL. We were so over-excited we opened a burn pool of the best Ben More clear water, and the Stagland birds went and pinched some of the Torosay daffys to eat with it. Isn't it wonderful.

We were very sad for one old stag who looks like being a switch. Every time he saw his picture in the pool, he put his foot in the water to make ripples and rub it out, in the hopes that some points would appear when the water calmed down again, but they never did.

Next morning was Church-day. (We always have Opening of Stag Parliament on Church-day as the horrible hunters are not supposed to go horrible hunting on Church-day). We all got up very early and lick polished ourselves all over, especially our toes which come up in a lovely shine and show up well in the sun when we Stag Jog. We put bits of white heather round our necks, formed up in three ranks with big stags on the end and little stags in the middle, and when Niall said 'Jog', we jog-trotted down the hill, singing the Stag Jogging song. Do you remember it, Henry?

One Two, One Two,
ALL Stags move, not-just-a-few.
Knees up, Knees up,
Old or young – never give up.
Jog along, Jog along,
As you sing this-happy-song.
Left up, Right up,
Back and Front,
Head up, Tail up,
Smile and Grunt, Smile and Grunt.

*… Bowing his head to the ground …*

The sun was just rising, and we reached Laggan Forest in time for Mossie-breakfast. We took our own as there is still a shortage of good grass over there.

When we arrived we were met by a very smart young Usher-stag. He was wearing a birch leaf on each horn and greeted us by putting one front foot over the other and bowing his head to the ground, giving a wag with his tail as he did so. With a little grunt he jogged ahead of us to our place on a ledge near the top of the corrie. He jogged beautifully and his toes shone so well in the rising sun. Niall arranged us on the rocks so that we could all see, then he left us to join the Councillors down by the burn. There were already many, many smell sentries round the top of the corrie, so we did not have to bother and could just relax and wait for Parliament to assemble below by the burn. Rory was with The Monarch as his page, so we hadn't seen him since the day before.

Herds of stags and herds of hinds came in from every corner and were given lying positions all round the corrie. Yes, Henry, the hinds came too because this is such an important day in Stagland. After the Opening of Stag Parliament, the hinds all go off to their private nest places, high up in the hills, to have their babies.

Then slowly the birds of Stagland assembled above us with their twig radios, waiting to report the events to all the wildlife world and, at the same time, to watch out for any horrible hunters who should have been in church and were not.

There was a long, long wait, Henry, and we all got worried in case The Monarch had got stag-flu or something. At last, when the sun was fully up, and the sky was blue as blue, and a flying jumbo overhead, we saw, away down the glen, The Monarch's procession, and we could just hear the big twee-grunting choir singing The Monarch's marching song:

The Monarch's the stag for me,
Tee-he, Tee-he, Tee-he.

He sees that we are all free,
Tee-he, Tee-he, Tee-he,
To do what we like
To ride on a bike
Or jump in the deep blue sea – he-he!

The procession came closer and closer, led by two big police stags, then the twee-grunting choir, then two lines of young smell-sentries with The Monarch between them, and behind the Monarch – what do you think, Henry? – yes, it was – it was Rory dancing a little jig as he came along, polishing the Monarch's back with lick polish as he danced. His toes were so brightly polished that the peat wouldn't even stick to them. And behind him, one or two old hinds with special smelling moss and stag bandages in case The Monarch felt icky. (They had purple heather crosses on their backsides.)

I must stop there, Henry as G. E. P. (Golden Eagle Post) is gliding this way. He hasn't been very well last two days, but he says he will manage to make Fossoway tonight as the wind is behind him. You may have to let him perch on Fred's kennel for the night if he is too weary – and have some cod liver oil ready for him.

Your old chum,

Alby

*Lick polishng*

Hello Henry! Are you still jogging like me?

# Letter No. 15 from Alby to Henry

TELEPHONE
STAGLAND 303

SOMEWHERE ON THE ISLE OF MULL
ARGYLL
SCOTLAND
30th May

HULLOOO, Henry,

Are you still jogging Henry? I hope so. Next time you go jogging, whistle the jogging song, and I'll see if I can hear you.

You remember I was telling you about the Opening of the Stag Parliament in my last letter. The Monarch's procession had appeared at the bottom of the corrie and everyone seemed set to receive him.

All the Professors were sitting on a small mound and the various Stag-Councils were gathered round the big stone where the Monarch was going to sit. Our Council, with Niall in the front, did not have a very good place. They were right behind those great big stags from CAIRN BAN. Niall was very upset but he had drawn the shortest bit of heather when they cast lots for places, so he was bound to have the last place.

At the bottom of the corrie, on a stone in the burn, stood a booful highly polished stag, with stag moss of every colour hung round him, and a thin stick in his mouth.

This was the Lord-Stag-Chamber-Lain awaiting his master, The Monarch. He is really the boss of all The Monarch's helpers, Henry, and when he is with The Monarch he has to put on all his ribbons, and is only allowed to walk backwards.

When the procession reached the Lord-Stag-Chamber-Lain, he bowed to the ground and gave a wag with his tail. The twee-grunters stopped singing, the police stags and the smell-sentries

*… We all stood up, bowed and wagged our tails …*

drew aside, and The Monarch issued a HUGE GRUNT which could be heard all across the corrie.

We all stood up, bowed and wagged our tails. The Stagland birds all tweeted, and in the distance, when all was quiet, we could hear 'Cuckoo-cuckoo' and the bark of Trash as he watched from afar.

Slowly the Lord-Stag-Chamber-Lain walked backwards, followed by the Monarch walking forwards, followed by Rory with his head held high, going a little red with embarrassment, as he lick polished The Monarch's back every ten yards.

On reaching the big stone, The Monarch climbed on to it, turned and gave another mighty grunt. Then the Head Professor came forward and bowed to The Monarch and pushed a slate in front of it with Stag writing on it. The Lord-Stag-Chamber-Lain gave three little grunts, facing a different direction each time he grunted, and many hundreds of deer grunted back, and we then listened carefully to all The Monarch grunted out.

I won't bore you with all the things he said, Henry, but it was very interesting, telling us what Stag Parliament was going to do during the next year.

When he was finished, he looked all round the corrie so that we could see his wonderful head while Rory went on lick-polishing his back.

*… Finally, he went back to the bottom of the corrie, stood on the big stone and gave out more big grunts …*

Then, The Monarch went round all the herds on the side of the corrie with the Lord-Stag-Chamber-Lain and Rory, grunting happy messages as he went and wishing the hinds happy baby time. Finally he went back to the bottom of the corrie, stood on his big stone and gave one more big grunt and rejoined his procession. The choirs were already singing The Monarch's Marching Song and moving off. As the sound of the singing faded away, we could see the procession entering the woods where The Monarch has his mossy home.

After they had gone, we all stag-jogged back to Ben More. It was a very happy day, Henry, and The Monarch looked so wonderful, and Rory was such a good boy and so proud of his horns – I felt quite worn out at the end of it all. Now I must go and post this on the Scots Fir Branch as G. E. P. is getting very idle these days and never comes to collect the letters. It's over-excitement at the thought of his baby chicks!

Night night, Henry

## Alby

*The Lord-Stag-Chamberlain*

# Letter No. 16 from Alby to Henry

TELEPHONE
STAGLAND 303

SOMEWHERE ON THE ISLE OF MULL
ARGYLL
SCOTLAND
6th June

Oh, Henry! Oh, Henry!

A terribly sad thing happened the other day – soon after we all got back from the Opening of Parliament. I had just got up in the morning and was taking a stroll along the top of the birch tree grove by the Mossieburn, looking for a good dew-grass breakfast, when I smelt something – something very strong and very horrible. It was a mixture between best whisky, old tartan and stale tobacco, and when I looked towards where I smelt, I saw the nastiest sight. Lying on a small bank on the edge of the birch trees were two men – one was the new head of horrible hunters on the Estate, and the other was his 'guest'. The 'guest' was dressed in tartan plus-fours, with a tartan cap, a tartan cover for his rifle, smoking a pipe filled from a tartan tobacco pouch.

He was telling the head of horrible hunters that he had shot hundreds and hundreds of stags in his wonderful country where they were much bigger than us. I heard him say that he reckoned he was the best rifle shot in the world. He was really horrible, Henry, and he hadn't shaved either! And then, oh, Henry! – and then I saw, coming out of the Birch tree grove, Ronnie the Roe's half-brother, who has got the most lovely head – he's a lovely fellow altogether. He was in real danger, Henry, and only about 200 yards from the hunters, AND he wasn't smelling where he was going. The poor Roe never have smell-sentries, they have to smell their own danger, and if they are busy eating dew-grass breakfast, they often forget to smell, and Ronnie's half-brother had forgotten to smell!

Well, Henry, the hunters didn't see Ronnie's half-brother for a moment or two but suddenly the head of horrible hunters saw him. He gave the 'guest' a clout on the nut and whispered to him to shut-up and look. Then he took the rifle out of the tartan case and gave it to the 'guest', at the same time pointing to where Ronnie's half-brother was. The 'guest' was so excited that the smell of best whisky, old tartan and stale tobacco got stronger and stronger. He pulled himself round so that he was lying on his front facing Ronnie's half-brother, and aimed the rifle, but he couldn't keep it steady. I could see the front of it going round and round. No way was he going to hit Ronnie's half-brother. He was so excited, Henry, and his hand wouldn't stay still as he had drunk so much whisky and smoked so much tobacco. Knowing that he would get a large tip if the 'guest' got that lovely head to take back to his own country and hang over his loo, the head of the

*… You have never seen such a carry on …*

horrible hunters seized the rifle from the 'guest's' hands, aimed and fired. The bullet got Ronnie's half-brother right in the middle of the head, and he fell to the ground. The great thing was, Henry, that the head of the horrible hunters really was a good shot, and Ronnie's half-brother never even knew what had hit him. If the 'guest' had fired, he might have hit him in the tum or anywhere, and that would have been really horrible.

Well, Henry, you have never seen such a carry-on that followed. The hunter and his 'guest' walked up to their 'prize'. The 'guest' produced a bottle of Glenlivet from his tartan holdall, poured some of it over the Roe's head, some of it down the hunter's throat and the rest down his own throat. Then he started to dance a jig, screaming and yelling as he danced round Ronnie's half-brother's body. After he had done this for about five minutes, I was so pleased to see him trip on a twig and fall flat on his face in a bit of the mossie bog. You would have laughed, Henry. When he got up, his face was all mud, the tartan colours were all running into each other, his bottle of Glenlivet had burst, and all that was left of that filthy pipe was the mouthpiece which had got stuck in his false teeth, AND he was crying like a baby. The hunter had to calm him down after he had pulled out a radio telephone and called for help.  .

About fifteen minutes later, there was a loud rattling noise in the birch trees, and a huge tracked vehicle appeared, like a house on tracks. It had lovely cushions in the back for the 'guest', with a cocktail bar and hot thermoses full of stew. There was a rack in the front for the deer-bodies, and a seat beside the driver for the hunter. It had a wireless aerial with a foreign flag flying from the top of it, and a stereo playing trumpet marches!

It was pulling a toilet-trailer which had a shower, a Turkish bath and a loo with a big stag's head hanging over it. What a machine, Henry. A smart-looking chap got out of the toilet-trailer and offered the 'guest' a towel to wipe the mud off his face and a cup of hot stew from a thermos. The hunter loaded Ronnie's half-brother's body onto the rack in front, the 'guest' got onto the soft cushions, his helper returned to the toiler-trailer, the hunter got in with the driver, and the vehicle disappeared back into the trees. That's the sort of thing we have to put up with nowadays on Ben More, Henry! Rory saw most of it happening, and it has taught him a lesson, to always smell where he is going otherwise he, too, might end up on the rack of that dreadful vehicle.

I'm off for my holiday tomorrow, Henry. Niall and I are going to the South of Mull to get the sun and see some relations. We'll only be away two weeks. I have asked Rory to drop you a short note each week to tell you what is happening – I hope he remembers. I have also told G. E. P. to remember to call for Rory's note.

Be a good boy Henry – Your old friend,

# Letter No. 1 from Rory to Henry
## (No 17 from Mull)

TELEPHONE
OUT OF ORDER!

SOMEWHERE ON THE ISLE OF MULL
ARGYLL
SCOTLAND
13th June

Hi-de-Hi-Henry – Henry, Rory here – Rory here Henry.

Hope you are OK and being good boy like me, Henry.

Henry, my Dad and his Dad have gone skunning off to the South of Mull for sun and fun. Granddad Alby told me I had to right to you each week and keep in touch – so, Henry, I went to see the Professor and asked him to see if my letter was OK. He has corrected sum of my mistakes but, as u see, not orl of them!

By the way, Henry, I am so proud of the six points I'm going to have this year. I long to have ten points wun day, but the Professor says I never will as I am such a bad adder. Please cum and help teech me how to do it, Henry. You see, my trouble is that wen I get to nine, I always go back to wun – because I have no more numbers. Two, three four, five, sicks, seven, ate and nine, have orl gone. Professor says 'go back to wun and add nuthing' – well, I do that like a good boy, Henry, but I've still got wun because that's what wun and nuthing cum to. Anyway, I'll lern wun day.

You know, Henry, wen me Dad and Granddad went orf, plus sum of their chums, I thort I would be all kind of free to do what I liked, and I planned to go down to Bunessan and dig those naughties out for a bit of romp around. Well, I did go down, and I did dig them out, but somehow I thought I'd better take them back to Ben More as there wasn't too many smell-sentries left about. I suddenly felt rather important and responsible, Henry, with me Dad and Granddad

52

away. The three of us went back and all took our turn at smell-sentries, and we lick polished ourselves each morning, and we went to Church-day Service, and we, all three, tried to behave like big boy stags – it was rather fun, and I fink (oh bother) ... think the rest of the heard preciated us.

There was wun funny moment, Henry. The boys and me went for a frolick down the glen one evening when we was – were – off dooty. As we were running down hill, we passed an old hind all nestled in a green patch, waiting to have her baby. Beside her was her two-year-old daughter,

who was very booful. Anyway, as we run by, the old lady got up and trotted off. The daughter looked back at me, Henry. (The nobbers say she was looking at them, but she wasn't – she was looking at my luvely six points all still wrapped up in velvet – I promise she was, Henry – these nobbers – it's just conseet, that's what they've got).

She was booful, very booful. She had lick polished her coat all over so you could see your horns in it and her toe nails was polished like jooels. She had two little whiskers, Henry, sticking out by her mouth, and she whiskered them from side to side and showed her luvely clean teeth and waved her ears – and what eyes, Henry! I felt like a myxie rabbit and got fright in case the Golden Eagle Post should swoop and eat me up as petrol.

I let those stoopid nobbers watch as I did my best stag-jog over to where the hinds were standing – not a shot's distance from where they had been lying. I grunted the jogging song, and I must have looked very good 'cause the young hind started walking my way, with eyes gleamed like dye-amonds. Oh, she was booful, Henry. I grunted He-e-ello, and she grunted back Hee-ee-loah. Oh, it was luvely, Henry, but the old lady suddenly saw us and gave out a bark like nine

*Golden eagle post coming in for the mail*

orlsations and charged me. Henry, I promise I have never run faster. I took off down the hill, followed by the naughties, laughing their silly little sides off.

When we got to the burn, the naughties started to rag me, telling me I was becoming a dandy six pointer just trying to attract the girls, so I stood up on my back legs, Henry, and challenged them each to a front-foot boxing match. I gave them 'Dandy Six Pointer' orl right, Henry. They both had two black eyes by the time I had finished but I had a broken toe nail which was a bit sore going back up the hill.

Anyway, we're all good friends again, and back on smell-sentry together. We mustn't mind having our leg pulled, must we, Henry? I'm sure you don't.

I was given a new Stagshot-two-snaptaker for my last birthday and thort you might like this wun of Golden Eagle Post cumming in for the mail last week.

The old bird's in great form, Henry. He is so proud of his new Eaglets but I'm rather afraid Mrs Golden Eagle may be pinching one or two of Mr MacTavish's lambs for brecky – tee – and – dinner. She better watch out or she'll get a pellet in her pullover.

'Hi – come here – G. E. P., here's Henry's letter – thank you.'

Bi-Bi for now, Henry

Your partner in crime

Rory

# Letter No. 2 from Rory to Henry

## (No. 18 from Mull)

SOMEWHERE ON THE ISLE OF MULL
ARGYLL
SCOTLAND
20th June

Hi-ye, Henry – Rory here.

What terrible weather we're having for the time of year. Wunder if it's as bad with you at home.

It's very wet on the sides as we sit on smell-sentry for hours on end. You see, Henry, sum more stags have gone on hols so there are very few of us left for smell-sentry duty. Anyway there's nuthing to smell except toorist, and they do smell strong and nasty, Henry.

Wun day last week. I was torking to the naughties on smell-sentry when we got the most awful townie whiff. Sort of washing-machine-soda-mixed-with-new-linen-shorts smell. The party came into site about two rifle shots below us. There was a Dad and Mum and three two-legged nobbers. They had a big black and white curly dog and a horrid little yapping terrier. Dad was in front, then Mum, then the three little fellows. They all had things like bicycles on their backs with colour tents and other toys tied on to them. The dogs were bounding about like what they owned the place. Dad was smoking a great big pipe with smoke cumming out of the front, and they all looked like the Cween Elizabeth sailing down the Sound.

Well, Henry, you smell all sorts in this world but we all thought this was the bottom. We watched them go over the brow, then saw them cum up the other side of the glen. Then they stopped, sat down and took their bicycle-like things off their backs. They unpacked bags, and those horrid dogs started chasing Mr MacTavish's sheep. Then, Henry, you wouldn't believe it – they lit a fire in the heather and there was smoke everywhere. Ignorant idiots.

56

I thought of my Dad and Granddad – they wouldn't like this very much. It was my duty to go and see them off, even if they turned out to be dangerous – me with my six points, I couldn't sit down and do nothing. I lick polished myself all over, got one of the naughties to blow the cobwebs off the velvet on my six points and stag-jogged off down the hill. I went round the back of them so that I could give them a fright as I came over the hill behind them. The smoke was something orful. Just as I was getting close, those two dogs came chasing over the hill, yapping no-how. They thort they would frighten me, but they didn't, Henry. You know what, Henry, I got a left and right with my back feet – two kicks, one with each foot got each dog fair and square of the nose, and Henry did they yelp! The dogs ran back to their master just over the hill, screaming like dying pigs. I walked slowly on. The smell was absolutely 'gusting – much worse than the horrible hunters. I looked over the ridge and there they were mopping up the blood on their two little dears' noses.

*… I got very close and then they saw me …*

I got very close, and then they saw me. You have never seen anything so funny, Henry, they dropped everything and ran across the peat bogs and heather as fast as they could, falling over, getting up, saying nasty things, and the dogs' noses still bleeding. I stamped out the fire and followed.

After about ten minutes they came to a rock on the next ridge. They were panting and blowing. Suddenly, from behind the rock, came the naughties who had been watching. Then the rest of the herd, then Trash the sheep dog, then Mr MacTavish, then the Golden Eagle Post and all the birds of Stagland flew overhead. The Townies were terrified, Henry. They lay in a bog with their hands up, begging for their lives, and asking what they had done to deserve all this. Just as Mr MacTavish was about to tell them, Henry, the most wonderful thing happened.

High, high up – 36,000 feet up – a flying Jumbo changed course and wrote a message with its vapour trail.

'THOU SHALT NOT LIGHT FIRES ON THE HILLS OR LEAVE LITTER ABOUT OR THOU SHALT BE HAUNTED BY THE ANIMALS AND BIRDS WHOSE HOME THEY ARE'

As the vapour trails faded away, the deer and the birds and Mr MacTavish and Trash faded away as well, leaving the townies lying in the peat bog covered in mud. They were just recovering from their terrible shock when they looked up and saw another flying Jumbo going the other way. It just left one word of vapour in the sky:

'UNDERSTAND?'

I don't know whether they did understand or not, Henry.

Anyway, G. E. Post is going to take this over tomorrow after my Granddad Alby has seen it – he comes back on the new moon tonight next week he will tell you about his holiday.

Do you think I'll ever be a Royal, Henry? It's easier to count twelve than ten because twelve has no 'nuthing' in it.

Chin – chin, old chappie,

Rory

# Letter No. 17 from Alby to Henry

## (No 19 from Mull)

TELEPHONE
STAGLAND 303

SOMEWHERE ON THE ISLE OF MULL
ARGYLL
SCOTLAND
27th June

Hello Henry, Hello – Hello – Hello,

I'm back from my hols in the South of Mull, and Rory tells me he has been a good boy and written to you each of the two weeks I have been away. I saw one of his letters, and it looked all right even if the spelling did go astray every now and again.

Well, Henry, the first week Niall, myself and three young nobbers did a tour of Mull, ending in the South by the sea.

We visited nearly every stag herd on the Island and paid our respects to the Monarch, who is getting rather old and crotchety now. We met many, many hinds on our travels all in their baby-nests hidden from as much as they could be hidden from. Many of them already had their babies – very booful they are with white spots.

We saw Rory's Mummie, Morag, who has got twin nobbers – that makes ten sons and never a daughter. She says she's not going to have any more babies after this year so we told her the horrible hunters would soon make sausages out of her if that was the case. She said they would be jolly tough sausages, and the horrible hunters would break their teeth on them, and that would teach them not to be nasty to old ladies.

Our last call was at the herd of the big stags of Cairn Ban. They were very kind to us, and some of them took us out for a lovely dinner of sun-heated-juniper with salt-watersauce. Then they took us to the Fairies' Circle at the end of Loch Don. They told us the story how hundreds and

*… A litle boy had wished for a saddle …*

hundreds of years ago, there were terrible stag herd battles there, and many a big stag lay buried in the big mound as in those days there were no humans about to make sausages of them. They showed us the Circle of Stones where the fairies come when the moon is full to guard the big stags' spirits, and they told us that if we all sat in the middle of the circle and made a wish, it would be granted after the next full moon. We all sat down and wished.

Niall asked them who the last person was to make a wish, and they said that two moons ago a little boy had wished for a saddle for his pony, and one moon ago he came to the circle and found one covered in grass.

The big stags told us we must not tell anyone what we had wished for until the next moon so I'm sorry, Henry, but I can't tell you what I wished for – I will one day.

*… As we paddled 'mongst the seaweed …*

After that, we moved on South until we were lying on the beach opposite Iona it was very lovely. It may have been somewhere there that St Columba landed on Mull for the first time, over fourteen hundred years ago, when he brought the story of Stag Jesus to Scotland, but some people think he landed for, the first time near the Fairies' Circle at Loch Don.

Anyway, we all felt very peaceful and happy as we paddled 'mongst the seaweed and the baby crabs and the pebbles.

On the tenth day of our holiday, the most wonderful thing happened. A helicopter suddenly appeared over Iona Abbey. It came lower and closer every minute. There were only five of us there, and we all got a little frightened. We thought it might be full of horrible foreign hunters with machine guns or something – so we all hid behind rocks. Can you believe it, Henry, the helicopter landed on the sands just where we had been lying and out got a very important looking chap, who certainly didn't look like a horrible hunter. He came towards our rocks, and I went out to meet him. I grunted when he got close and with a charming smile, he said:

'Can you please tell me where I can find a stag called "Alby" – a ten pointer I think.'

'I am Alby,' I said, 'and I am about to become a Royal.'

'Oh,' said the gent, 'How do you do? I'm Henry's Uncle Christopher, and our team helped your grandson, Rory, to escape in the Sound of Mull a few weeks back.'

It was wonderful to meet him, Henry, and I thanked him for all he had done. Then the other four of our party came out from behind the rocks, and I introduced them.

Uncle Christopher said he had just taken one of his customer's secretary all the way from London to the Isle of Arran with his mail and was now on his way back. He wanted to know whether Niall and I would like a day in London at his expense – what a wonderful offer. We talked to the other three of our party about it. They all said that we must go and that they would find their own way back to Ben More.

Uncle Christopher led Niall and I to the helicopter and told us to get in the back seat and put our heads through the sunshine roof. He told us not to put our horns too high otherwise they would be cut off by the rotor blades.

We did all this. It was very exciting, Henry, but rather frightening. The rotor blade started. It went faster and faster and faster, and I could feel the draught taking the velvet off my horns. We sat very still and at last we took off. We went up and up and the wind was so strong we started to cry. Below our three friends stood on their hind legs and waved us goodbye with the front ones.

Uncle Christopher started saying funny things down a funny looking object in front of him. Then he shouted up to us and said:

'I've got two stalls for you in a five-star Animotel. It's called Zoo.'

Here comes dear old G. E. Post. I hope he's not eating too many of Hamish's lambs.

More next week,

Alby

# Letter No. 18 from Alby to Henry

## (No. 20 from Mull)

TELEPHONE
STAGLAND 303

SOMEWHERE ON THE ISLE OF MULL
ARGYLL
SCOTLAND
4th July

Hello Henry,

I must go on with my holiday story. Remember we had just taken off in the Uncle's helicopter with our heads sticking out of the sunshine roof – ooh, it was cold Henry, and our heads shook like tattie riddles as that rotor went round and round above us. Anyway, three hours later we landed at a place called Batter Sea, and the Uncle had a lovely stag trailer waiting with a Rolls Royce to pull it. It pulled us all the way to our five star Animotel, called 'zoo'. Here we were met by the manager, who was very friendly and said we would be in cages 226 and 228, next to the reindeer because he thought we might have a lot in common. Silly nit! Reindeer speak Norwegian and their stags are called bulls – we had nothing the same except that we did both eat hay – and, Henry, we tucked into plenty of that after the long cold flight.

Uncle Christopher wished us 'Goodnight' and said he would be back after mid-day hay-time next day – he was sure the manager would look after us.

He did. We were called in the morning by two penguins in their white shirts and tails, with a beak-full of rather tough dew-grass. Then, the manager came along and asked if we would like to earn a little money to spend on our London Holiday. We said 'Yes,' and we were told we would have saddles put on our backs and townie nobbers would give us some money for a ride round 'zoo'. We made a lot of money, Henry, but is was terrible. The townie brats squealed, and their mums squealed too, in case we would eat them. I think they thought we were lions or tigers!

In the afternoon, Uncle Christopher came along with all of his family. He wished us happiness and vanished. The cousins were very kind and first took us to see the Chamber of Horrors which is close to zoo but we thought ordinary life in London was bad enough without making it worse.

When we came out, everyone kept looking at us, and we were both getting a little embarrassed so the cousins decided to take us to the cinema to see Mickey Mouse. That was all right except

that, as soon as we sat down, the wifey behind started creating because she couldn't see. She asked us to take our horns off.

When the cinema had finished, we started to walk back to zoo, but it was really very hot, so the cousins said they would take us on a bus. Well, we both put out our front legs and a Number 10 stopped (poor Rory wouldn't have known what number it was – he can only count to nine – remember?) We climbed on board, and the conductor said 'No deer inside – only on top' – so we climbed the stairs but there was no room, so Auntie asked what we should do. 'Climb on to the roof,' the conductor said – so we climbed. It was hard to hang on but we did, and all the people on the pavements cheered and waved to us.

There was one bad moment when we went under a bridge. I thought we were going to be knocked off the bus top, but we saw it in time and lay very flat with our horns lying over the side of the bus in case they got hurt.

Anyway, we got back to zoo – thanked the cousins – had some dry hay and went to ziss. In the morning, Uncle Christopher came with his trailer and took us back to Batter Sea, and we got into the helicopter which was already loaded with 'the customer's' secretary and one 13p letter.

Another terrible three hours bouncing about, with our heads out of the sunshine roof
– AND it was raining.

When we landed at Arran, the 'customer' came out with his friend and an elephant rifle.

'Good heavens, Christopher,' he said, 'Do you realise you've got two stags on board?'

'Absolutely,' said Uncle Christopher, 'They're on their way to Mull.'

'Should hope so,' said the customer, 'Don't want little rags like that on Arran.'

'What cheek – shall we chase him now or later?' said Niall.

I told him to keep quiet otherwise we might get left on Arran – a fate worse than sausages. We sat there terrified we might never take off – but we did, and the Uncle put us down nicely on the top of Ben More. We thanked him very, very much indeed and offered him a best-Mossieburn-dinner but he said he, had to get back, and left as the whole herd stood on their hind legs and gave the famous Ben More Deer Clap with their front legs.

Now I know why townies' smell is so awful, Henry.

Here comes Ronnie the Roe. He says he's been chased by that horrible hunter in the tank all week and has been missed twice. He also says that Hamish is after G. E. Post as his lambs are disappearing. So this letter is being taken all the way to you by Gorkie the Grouse who, incidentally, married Miss Partridge in the end, and she has hatched six beautiful little Part-Grise.

Somehow we must all help Ronnie to escape from that horrible hunter. I'll tell you more next week.

Be a good boy now, Henry – I hope you are still doing your jogging. I haven't heard you shouting 'ALBEEE – ALBEEE' for a long time – have a go now.

Your old friend,

# Letter No. 19 *from* ALBY *to* HENRY
## (21 *from* Mull)

TELEPHONE
STAGLAND 303

SOMEWHERE ON THE ISLE OF MULL
ARGYLL
SCOTLAND
11th July

Hello Henry,

Poor old Gorkie the Grouse came back from your home very tired last week – he hadn't flown so far without seeing any heather for years, and he said your letter was very heavy. Anyway, he's back with his Partridge wife and their little Part-Grise babies so all is well. It's good to know, too, that Golden Eagle Post is not playing with his babies so much now, and will be back on his job as postman this week. Mrs Golden Eagle will join him as soon as her two babies have flown from the Eyrie. (That's a Golden Eagle's nest, Henry).

As the Summer weeks and months go past, the horrible hunters get more active, and we all have to be very alert to avoid becoming 'roast-grouse-and-bread-sauce' or 'roastvenison-and-red-currant-jelly' or even just 'sausages'. The hunters haven't started hunting us stags seriously yet but there is always some 'nasty' that wants one of us for juicy venison stew at this time of year, and there are many prepared to pay a lot of money to take home a lovely roe-deer head to put over the loo. The wonderful thing is, Henry, that all the birds and beasts of Stagland help each other to take care.

Last week Roger the Raven went down to the coast to see who was using the ferries. He saw that stupid man in his tank-caravan-thing with Ronnie's poor half-brother's beautiful head nailed to the front of it. He was trying to drive on to the Fishnish Ferry, but the tank-thing got stuck on the ramp and caused an awful jam. When it did manage to go backwards, there was a terrible 'bump', and bottles and bottles of Glenlivet broke all over the pier. It had to reverse all the way to Graignure and wait for the big ferry. No one in Stagland cared which ferry it went on as long as it went away.

While Roger was watching, he saw a young man ride off the ferry on a motor bike, with a rifle over his back, and reported this to Ben More by twig radio. This was bad news.

We don't like those townie youngsters on the island. All they think about is killing us and our friends, so we put out extra smell-sentries for protection.

It was just after dawn next day when we were all watching Ronnie the Roe way below us in a glade in the Mossieburn birch trees. He was whistling his mating tune and chasing Mona, his girl friend, round and round in circles. Every now and again he stopped and made 'Come-and-talk-to-me-looks' at Mona and she made 'No-I-won't-looks' at Ronnie. Then, a little while later, Mona would get in the centre of the circle and flutter her eyelids and wriggle her nose and look at the ground, making 'Come-and-talk-to-me-signs' to Ronnie, but when that happened, Ronnie would just go on whistling.

Well, Henry, while all this was going on, one of our smell-sentries had seen that smart young man on his motor bike, going along the road below.

When he was immediately below us, he turned into the hill, and we couldn't see him any more, although we could hear the bike. The noise got louder and louder, and then it stopped – somewhere below where Ronnie and Mona were. Ronnie just went on whistling – he wasn't paying any attention to his smell-senses, but we were. Suddenly the lowest down smell-sentries stood up, then Niall stood up, then we all stood up. The smell of townie-smart-young-man was unmistakable. Then we saw him – oh, Henry! He wasn't half a rifle shot from Ronnie lying on the bank, looking at Ronnie through his telescope. Ronnie and Mona were having an awful row about which way to run round the circle, and anyway they were upwind from the young man so couldn't smell him. We saw the rifle come out of the case. We saw its safety catch moved. We saw the rifle being put to the shoulder. We saw the finger fingering the trigger. We didn't know what to do, Henry. Then, suddenly, Niall grunted – 'Gallop'. We all, yes all 50 of us stags, galloped down the hill, Henry, as fast as we could, and we all jumped over the young man. The rifle went 'Bang' as Niall, who was leading, jumped.

Ronnie jumped too – about ten foot into the air as the bullet went underneath him. Then he and Mona galloped off with us through the birch trees. The young man was so frightened by our stampede that he couldn't reload.

After we had gone a little way, we all stopped and got our breath back. Ronnie and Mona were still with us. They had had a terrible fright.

A smell-sentry walked slowly back to see what the young man was up to. He found him down the hill trying to start his motor cycle but it had been lying in the damp and wouldn't go. Eventually he stumped off towards the road in a rage, leaving the bike propped up against a birch tree.

After he had gone, we all went back to look at the dreadful machine. Rory said he knew all about bikes. He once saw Constable Donald kicking his new one to make it go. He smelt all round the bike, then we all smelt round it, then Ronnie and Mona smelt round it.

Mona said she remembered her mother riding a pedal bike years and years ago, and thought she knew how it was done. She said she would have a try on this one if the stags would push her. And so the two big police stags held the bike up while Mona got on. Then they pushed her along. Suddenly Rory jogged up and kicked it with his back feet. Well, Henry, what do you think? There was a bang and the engine started, and Mona and the bike hurtled down the hill. Mona couldn't get her front leg off the horn so the noise was terrible. On and on she went. We went after her to see what was going to happen. As she was getting close to the road at the bottom of the hill she passed the young man, who pulled his rifle off his back and tried to aim it. Mona leapt into the air, crashed into a peat bog and rushed back to join us with at least three bullets following her.

The bike went on on its own, Henry, going faster and faster until it hit the road just as a large van carrying the supplies for the Duart Castle tea-room was coming round the corner. The van got the bike amidships. That was the last we saw of the bike or the young man, Henry.

We all climbed back to the top of the Ben and put out our smell-sentries once more. Ronnie and Mona came halfway up the hill then trotted off into the bracken to be together.

Golden Eagle Post swooped down for the letter and said he had seen the whole story from the top of the biggest birch tree. He said he had shaken half his feathers out with laughing. Maybe the young man will become a stockbroker and take up golf. He would be safer that way, don't you think so, Henry?

Until next week

Alby

# Letter No. 20 from Alby to Henry

## (22 from Mull)

TELEPHONE
STAGLAND 303

SOMEWHERE ON THE ISLE OF MULL
ARGYLL
SCOTLAND
18th July

Hello Henry,

I haven't heard you shout back for the last week or two!

The other morning, me and one or two chums went for a trampie over the forest to see what was doing. There seemed to be hinds and one-year-olds and new babies everywhere. There were also sad little groups of nobbers and young hinds who had been chased away by their mummies so that the new babies could have more attention and so that the older ones could start to learn to look after themselves. The older ones are going to have to go to Professor Red Deer's School next term for the first time.

There was one very unhappy moment. We had just met a hind and her baby and were passing the time of day with her when there was a sudden whoosh from behind. This was Golden Eagle Post diving down on us. I thought he wanted this letter so I grunted to him that it wasn't ready yet. He paid no attention but stuck his talons out and dived on the hind's baby. He was mad Henry, quite mad, and he looked so fierce and cruel, and he wouldn't go away, so I'll tell you what I did. I stood by the baby deer and the next time he swooped, I kicked out with my hind legs, and although I missed him, he went away. Five minutes later he came back and swooped again. Again I kicked out with my hind legs just as he was about to stick his talons into the baby. This time I got him right in the beak. He let out a terrible shriek and landed on a rock very close to the baby. His face was all blood, and he was crying, Henry. Yes, he was crying, Henry. I went over to him and asked whatever came over him.

*… He stuck out his talons and dived on the hind's baby …*

'I'm sorry, Alby', he said, 'so very sorry. You see, Alby, my wife is running short of myxie rabbits for our two babies, and I had to find something but, Alby, I didn't know it was you – hoo – hoo – blub, blub.'

Well, Henry, I told him that he must never, never touch a deer baby again or he would get both my feet in his snout, and I told him it didn't matter whether it was me or what stag-person saw him, he would get the same treatment! Babies have to be looked after, Henry, no matter whether they are deer babies or eagle babies or your sort of babies they are all dear deer-God's babies, even Freddie the fox's babies!

The hind got some wet moss and bathed Golden Eagle Post's cut cheek, then plugged the cut up with some fine heather fibres, and all was forgiven. Golden Eagle Post flew off to look for myxie rabbits or moussies or something and promised he would find me later to collect this letter.

After a while we continued our trampie along the side of the hill and stopped for some 'levenses quite high up from where we could see right down the glen. It was a lovely warm spot with some fresh lush grass.

While we were guzzling, one of my friends suddenly put his head up. There, down the glen, came Mr MacTavish, Hamish and several of their friends – all spread out in a line up the hill. In front of them were their dogs led by Trash. They were gathering the sheep, Henry, to clip the mummy-sheep and be sure all the lambs are marked so that no one can pinch them.

It was a lovely sight to watch. Trash and his doggie friends ran up and down the hill collecting every sheep they could find and gathering them all into one flock, which grew in size as they came along. By the time they got to us there must have been three or four hundred of them. We stood still because if we had moved, the flock might have taken fright and that would have ruined all the work the dogs had done, and they are such good friends to us, Henry.

After they had gone, we wandered on towards Coire Bheinn, where we had lunch and spent the rest of the day. It was very beautiful, and we saw lots of friends – or relations of friends – they all seemed to have babies – even Gorkie-the-grouse's second cousin had a lovely family of eight little grouselets. I can't wait to tell Gorkie!

So long, Henry,

Your Chum

Alby

# Letter No. 21 from Alby to Henry

## (No 23 from Mull)

TELEPHONE
STAGLAND 303

SOMEWHERE ON THE ISLE OF MULL
ARGYLL
SCOTLAND
25th July

Hello, Buffday boy, Henry – Hello, Hello, Hello

You want to know something, Henry? It was Rory's birthday last week too, and you have never known anything like the party he had. He was five years old, and his six points are beginning to look very smart, and he lick-polished his coat all the night before, and he made his bed early in the morning, and as the sun came up he danced round the stag herd singing little grunting songs.

At elevenses time, the two naughty nobbers arrived from the Bunessan herd, and one or two big boys from Cairn Ban and some very strange friends of Rory's who he met when I was away for my holiday. I think they come from the north-west of the Island. They have long hair, weak horns and dirty noses. We had all hoped that Morag would come, but she was too busy looking after her twins.

Everyone brought prezzies for Rory. Some brought a packet of green grass from the fields, some brought soft mud to clean the toes with. One nobber brought a lovely bit of 'special' heather for Rory to clean his nose with so that he can smell things further away. Then there were a lot of old horns for eating or for dancing over, or for blowing like flutes! Practically everything was tied up in a Rhubarb leaf with sello-heather round it. Everyone shook Rory by the horns and wished him. Many Happy Returns of the Day.

At stag-lunch time, the whole herd and the guests stag-jogged down to the Mossieburn, singing the jogging song. There they found Professor Red Deer with a wonderful acre of new green grass with plenty of Bog Myrtle in it, and further on a mass of blaeberries for pudding. He and his students had been fertilising the field for weeks.

We all put our noses to the ground and wagged our tails while the Professor grunted a little prayer of thanks to dear deer-God for all the lovely things we were going to eat. And then we guzzled, Henry, guzzled and guzzled and guzzled.

After we had guzzled the last blaeberry, the two naughty nobbers appeared in the middle of the herd with a big, huge, square cake. It was beautifully made by Mona, the roe, out of corn which the Stagland birds had pinched from Mr McTavish's farm. It had five cast stag horns stuck in it for Rory's five years, and it was covered in Rhubarb leaves to keep it fresh. The naughties put it in front of Rory who grunted a lot of 'Thank-yous', and then took the first big munch. Oooh, it was good. As he took the big munch, all the animals and the birds of Stagland came from behind the trees and from over the trees to wish Rory Happy Birthday. Even Freddie the Fox was there and poor old Golden Eagle Post swooped down beside me – he was still crying and saying he would never be nasty to babies again.

When the cake was finished, all the young started stag-dancing – some doing the horn dance – some did the fox trot (led by Freddie the Fox), and some were just stag-jogging round in circles. All this to a wonderful band of twee-grunters provided by Professor Red Deer and supported by all who were there.

*… There was a big party of townies …*

Everyone was so happy that they completely forgot to put out smell-sentries. In the middle of the dance, Ronnie the Roe came running in to say that there was a big party of townies in red, yellow and green coats climbing up through the trees. We had to do something quick, Henry, because you never know – they might have been horrible hunters in disguise. Professor Red Deer had a good idea. He grunted to us to stand absolutely still and not to move. We did, and do you know, Henry, all fifteen townies walked by us not 20 yards away, and never saw us. 'Don't move and you won't be seen' is a good motto.

After the townies had gone, we went on eating the bits and pieces: Rory ate too much and had to have a lie-down before he went for his night out with the naughties – but more of the night out in my next.

Meanwhile, Henry, I hope you had a lovely birthday party yourself, with heaps of wonderful presents. I sent you a small prezzy, knitted by Mona, the Roe Doe, but it was too heavy for Golden Eagle Post, so I took it down to the gate at Fishnish and left it on the road just inside, hoping that when the foresters come in the morning they will see it and post it on to you by the ordinary postman. I didn't put who it was from on the outside as no forester would do anything to help us. They think we eat all their beastly trees – as if we would! They are as tough as leather and taste of resin. Yet, now I come to think of it, I have eaten one or two in the winter, Henry!

Bye bye for now, old man – 5 is a great age.

Your much older friend

Alby

*… Rory and the naughties on Inchkenneth …*

# Letter No. 22 from Alby to Henry

## (No 24 from Mull)

TELEPHONE
STAGLAND 303

SOMEWHERE ON THE ISLE OF MULL
ARGYLL
SCOTLAND
1st August 1985

Oh, Henry,

It sounds as if Rory's night out was very rough but the only news I have comes from the birds of Stagland and Rory himself.

You remember Rory had a wonderful party at Mossieburn with Professor Red Deer, where we ate far too much. In the afternoon he went to sleep in the bracken all on his own and in the evening he rejoined the herd to collect the two naughties before leaving for the birthday-night-out.

Soon after sundown, the three of them headed down towards Fishnish. The moon was full so it was easy to see what was going on, and it was a lovely warm night. After a ten-minute jog, they got to the gate in the deer-fence. (The one they marched through in triumph after saving the castle caretaker.) The idea was to get through the gate somehow, then creep along the coast and have a dinner of really lush fertilised grass or turnips or even Torosay Thomsonii. But none of this happened because when they arrived at the gate, they found a barbecue party going on just the other side of the fence.

There were about 20 people roasting sausages and hamburgers and drinking fine Glenlivet, so they couldn't get out, Ooh, but it did smell good, and the three boys wondered how they could get a bite for themselves.

Eventually, one of the naughties had an idea.

'Let us pretend we are tame deer in a deer farm. We must make ourselves look very smart, then go down to the fence, make grunting noises to the barbecuans and maybe they will give us their leftovers,' said the naughty.

'Great;' said Rory, 'we'll try it.' And they did try it. First they found a pool looked at themselves in it and did a big job lick-polishing their coats. Then they peat-polished their toes, then they stag-jogged down to the gate, making little grunt-noises as they went. The barbecuans were struck dumb. They couldn't believe what they saw the other side of the wire gate.

After a short while, one big fat horrible looking female barbecuan said to her equally big fat horrible looking husband.

'Look at the poor dear deers. They are locked in by the farmer and can't get out – let's give them their freedom.'

'Good idea,' said her husband.

'Then get some pliers. Horace, so that we can open the wire,' said the wife. They cut a big hole in the gate, but the staggies never moved. They just looked. The barbecuans tried to tempt them out with salad but they wouldn't come – because it had suddenly occurred to them they might not get in again.

*… The other naughty collected a crate of Smiths Crisps …*

Then, without warning, one of the naughties made a dash for a bowl full of salad and brought it back inside the fence. Then the other naughty collected a crate of Smith's Crisps the same way. Then Rory dived through and got a bag of potatoes. Then the barbecuans started saying horrible things like 'We'll get you for this' and 'We'll send for the hunters'. They were getting very angry, so the nobbers picked up their loot and took it way up the hill where they had a real good tuck-in and starting grunting 'We belong to Benmore, good old Benmore Hill'.

It was just before dawn when they went down to Balnahard on the coast. The naughties said they had never been in a boat – neither had Rory – so they pushed the small ferry boat belonging to the little Island of Inchkenneth into the sea and got in, and started to row with their horns. But as they had to row with their heads pointing downwards, they got giddy and their bodies started to sway from side to side and, yes Henry, you are right – they upset – right in the middle of the Loch, and they had to swim for it. They swam up wind, as Professor Red Deer had taught them, and they ended up, not on Mull, but on Inchkenneth where there was one big house with no one in it and lots and lots of lovely grass. They ate and ate and ate and at last they went to sleep in some rough ground near the beach. The sun was well up and it was hot.

They were woken by dogs barking and men shouting. The sheep-ferry and shepherds had arrived, and they were going to gather the sheep off the island and take them to Mull.

There was no way out, they were bound to be caught. The island was so small. The shepherds got closer and closer to their little hideaway. Then two dogs came sniffing round them. They got up. The shepherds saw them but didn't seem to mind, and then, Henry, oh Henry, Trash came up woofing at Rory. Then the nobbers knew they would be all right. Hamish came over the wall

'Goodness me,' he said to Rory, 'whatever are you doing here?'

Rory gave two grunts.

One hour later the sheep ferry set sail for Mull. On board it had three shepherds, three dogs, 150 sheep and three very bloated young stags.

When they got to the mainland, the nobbers thanked the shepherd's so very much by kneeling on their front legs and wagging their tails. Then they set off up the hill to rejoin us at the top of the Ben. Later on the naughties went back to Bunessan.

What a buffday, Henry. I am so pleased Rory hasn't got another one for a year – he looked awful when he got back.

Come back and see us again before too long, Henry – the horrible hunting season will start again soon – we don't like that.

Your chum,

Alby

# Letter No. 23 from Alby to Henry

## (No 25 from Mull)

TELEPHONE
STAGLAND 303

SOMEWHERE ON THE ISLE OF MULL
ARGYLL
SCOTLAND
8th August

Hello, Hello Henry

This is Alby with the weekly news and, oh, Henry, it was nearly very bad this week. No, it wasn't hunters or townies, it was something worse – it was foresters – 'furiating foresters. What happened was this:

Roger, the Raven, told us by twig radio that there were a lot of lorries, loaded with fencing posts, wire, tree plants, big hammers and all sorts of other tools, arriving by the morning ferry from Oban. He also told us that he had heard two townies, dressed in blue striped trousers and bowler hats, talking to two rough looking foresters down by the gate in the fence. The foresters were telling the townies that they would be very glad to plant the bit of Ben More which the townies had just bought, but they would have to fence the ground off first and destroy all the deer inside the fence. They said that all the necessary equipment was arriving shortly from Oban.

Well, Henry, what cheek! Pinching more of our precious grass to put their beastly trees on so that they can get off their taxes (at least that is what Professor Red Deer says they do!).

Anyway, we asked Niall to consult his council as to what to do. The Council then consulted the Lord-Stag-Chamber-Lain, and the Lord-Stag-Chamber-Lain consulted the Monarch, who sent a message to all stag herds to help us get rid of the 'furiating foresters in any way we could. Niall then had a meeting of members of all the stag herds on the island, and this is what we did.

On Church-day evening, ten stags dug a large trench across the road just inside the fence. Then they put birch branches over the trench. Two smell-sentries stayed in the woods quite close, to see what happened in the morning. Sure enough, when the sun was well up, three large lorries arrived. The gates were unlocked and the lorries drove in. The smell-sentries could hardly hold their grunts as the lorries came on – on – on and them BUMP into the ditch. Oh, what a bump. The fencing posts fell off, and the drivers hit their noses against the windscreens. They were all terribly angry, Henry, and had to send for a crane to pull their lorries out.

While they were waiting for the crane, they went down to the pub at the roadside where the barbecuans were – remember? When they were there, Freddie, the Fox, with two of his cubs, Rory and the two naughties jumped into the lorries and ate all the sandwiches the foresters had brought for their lunch! The foresters were furious when they came back.

It was very late by the time the crane had pulled the lorries out and even later by the time the fencing posts and wire had been unloaded and laid in neat little heaps on the hill. There were masses of them – they were going to fence in most of the blaeberries below Mossieburn.

Late that night about 150 stags assembled on Ben More. As the moon rose we all stag-jogged down to where the fencing posts were, and before sun-rise, Henry, we had scattered all the fencing posts over the hill, and we had unwound all the wire so that the heather got properly tangled up in it – oh, it was fun!

After breaky time the 'furiating foresters came back in a van. The smell-sentries said they had never seen such angry two-legged people. One went down to telephone his boss, and the two others were heard to say that they hoped the blue-suited townies wouldn't come back before they had got the fence started – but they did, Henry. They came back that afternoon. It was raining a little, and they had umbrellas and were wearing wellingtons. They were very angry and told the 'furiating foresters that they would not get paid unless the fence was started by morning.

The foresters tried to collect all the bits and pieces throughout the night but they couldn't find the poles, and the wire was all stuck to the heather so in the end they went to bed until daybreak. We just watched from the top of the hill and grunt-laughed.

About the middle of the night Olly, the Owl, had a good idea. He thought of getting the help of a huge flock of swallows that had just arrived on the Island so he flew off to the Mossieburn trees where he found the King Swallow. Olly persuaded the King Swallow to help. He wasn't keen to start with, saying that the more trees there were, the more places there would be for his flock to perch on in future.

After breaky the next day, the 'furiating foresters and the blue-suited townies came back. Not very much had happened to the fence, and the townies were not pleased. Suddenly there was a noise like a gale of wind. The townies' bowler hats blew off, and the whole party fell to the ground

*… They had umbrellas …*

as 3,243 swallows dived on them, dropping all sorts of things as they did so. Then they flew away and came back again as soon as the party stood up. They did this ten times and after the tenth time they went high, high up in the air, and got into a formation which spelt out 'Go home townies and pay your taxes like good boys'.

The townies were so angry that they ran down the hill and fell into the lorry pit as they did so, covering their lovely blue suits with mud, while the 'furiating foresters got into their lorries and drove off, muttering that Mull was not for them.

We all thanked ally very much indeed and also the King Swallow, Golden Eagle Post missed the whole thing as he was teaching his eaglets to fly. One of the eaglets is going to take this to you tonight Henry. His Dad will show him the way.

Sleep well, old friend,

Yours always

# Alby

P. S. The monarch has sent a twig-telegram to all the stag herds on Mull, telling them how well they had done to get rid of the 'furiating foresters.

*. . . 3,243 swallows got into a formation which spelt out . . .*

# Letter No. 24 from Alby to Henry

## (No 26 from Mull)

TELEPHONE
STAGLAND 303

SOMEWHERE ON THE ISLE OF MULL
ARGYLL
SCOTLAND
15th August

Hello Henry,

How are you? OK? Give us a shout – as loud as you can. It's rather windy up here just now, and I couldn't hear you shout last week.

Remember I told you how Stagland had got rid of the 'furiating foresters? Well, Henry, worse this week.

You see, we had the twelfth of August on Monday, and the twelfth (or the glorious twelfth, as the horrible hunters call it) is the real beginning of the hunting season, and the horrible hunters all come out of their offices in new plus-four suits, made of Harris Tweed. Their wives have plus-fours as well, and they all have stalkers hats with big salmon flies in them, or loud checked caps stuck on the side of their heads. They have new brogue shoes with hob nails in the soles. They have whistles hanging round their necks and cartridge bags and game bags and polished shepherds crooks. They all think they look very 'Highland' and 'Sporting' and tough. But they don't, Henry – they look like a lot of office townies in fancy dress – and they are a perfect nuisance to all in Stagland from now until after New Year.

The hotels love them because they pay good money for their cosy beds, hot baths, steak and kidney puds, Glenlivet and somewhere to tell stories of how they tried to kill some poor Stagland birds or beast. So, from now on, we have to double our smell-sentries and twig-radio birds.

The scene in Stagland is changing too, because the hinds have all had their babies and are living in big herds like the stags, but not with them; and the stags horns are getting firmer and the velvet starting to fall off. All the baby birds are starting to fly, and the roe deer are not chasing each other as much as they have been. Gorkie the Grouse's relations (and there aren't many!) are flying about in families, or coveys, as the hunters call them – perhaps 6, 7 or 8 in a family. And, Henry, the heather is all out and the hills are purple – you must come and see them soon. But I must tell you about the weekend before the Glorious Twelfth.

Two days before the Twelfth it was a Saturday, and the evening ferries were full of townies who had come to hunt in Stagland. Most of them had yapping teenage kids all over-excited at getting their first 'blood'.

Twig-radio was very good and kept sending us messages as the hunters landed. Gorkie, the Grouse, knew that it was his relations they were after because the twelfth was on Monday, and we knew that too.

Most of the hunters brought Pointer dogs. They are either great big white brutes with brown spots, or setters – weak looking shaggy red dogs – or German Pointers – brown things with no tails. These dogs walk slowly in front of their masters, and when they smell the grouse family hiding ahead of them, they stop dead still – only their nostrils twitching from side to side. The hunters advance, and when the grouse birds can stand it no longer, they get up and fly. Then the hunters shoot and the hunting hounds – Labradors and spaniels – rush forward and bring back whatever has been shot. The hunters blow whistles at the dogs, and curse them, while they put more cartridges in their horrible guns in case any poor member of the grouse family has been left behind.

Well, Henry, Stag-Council have been working on plans to help Gorkie the Grouse for weeks and weeks and weeks, and they had some very good ideas. One was all to do with cheese because once a dog has eaten a bit of cheese (and dogs love eating cheese), he won't be able to smell Grouse birds again for quite a long time. So:

All through the picnic season, the smell-sentries had been watching where townie trippers had been having their picnics, and each night a party of young stags (including Rory and his friends) went to the picnic place and smelt around for cheesy packets or left-over pieces. They made a store of all the cheesy things they could find close to the rock where Gorkie sits. Then, as soon as the twig-radios had told Stagland the hunters had landed, Gorkie and some of his bird friends flew the cheesy pieces all over the hill and hid them in the purple heather.

At the same time, Gorkie told the grouse families to go to boggy bits of heather, have a grouse-bath in it and move away, leaving their scent in the boggy bit.

On the night of the eleventh, the hotel bars were full of rich townies having big dinners and Glenlivet with their coffee. The teenage kids were dreaming up all the grouse birds they were going to shoot the next day. The Mums were either joining in the excitement or planning how they would get their families' plus-fours dry and clean when the hunters came home.

There were one or two young girlfriends of the teenage kids who were wishing they hadn't come at all.

Roger the Raven and Harry the Hoodie, together with their young, were sitting on the chimney tops of the pubs listening to the talk, and sending messages back to the herd by twig-radio. The keeper-hunters were getting out their new plus-four suits and deciding what they were going to do with all the tips they would get from the townies, while the land-owners, who had let their ground to the townies, were praying that there would be plenty of grouse birds to shoot at otherwise they might not get their rent.

Oh, here comes Golden Eagle Post with his other eaglet, to show her the way to your home. I'll have to stop now and tell you what happened on the Glorious Twelfth in my next. Golden Eagle Post can't wait because, like everyone else in Stagland, he is very, very, very busy helping everyone else to help everyone.

From

# Alby
## and all on the High Tops

*... Roger and Henry listening in ...*

# Letter No. 25 from Alby to Henry

### (No 27 from Mull)

TELEPHONE
STAGLAND 303

SOMEWHERE ON THE ISLE OF MULL
ARGYLL
SCOTLAND
22nd August

Hello Henry,

There's only time for one Hello this week as we are all so very busy looking out for horrible hunters just now, and it will be like that until the end of the season.

You remember in my last I told you how a mass of townies had arrived on the Island to celebrate the Glorious Twelfth by potting at Gorkie the Grouse's relations, and I told you about the funny clothes and the Pointer dogs they had brought and the wee cheese we had all been collecting to confuse the Pointer dogs. Well:

On the morning of the Glorious Twelfth we were sitting on the top of Ben More with all our smell-sentries out. We had put the wee cheese bitties all over the hill, and the Grouse coveys had had their grouse-baths and moved on, leaving their scent behind them. The Stagland birds were all on watch with Twig Radios overhead.

At about five hours after daybreak, two big Land Rovers came along the road from Torosay and stopped just beside Craig. A party of townies and keeper-hunters got out. Some had guns, some had whistles and dogs on the end of leads, some had whistles and dogs not on the end of leads. Some were so small they could hardly walk through the heather.

As they were getting themselves organised, one of the young ones looked at us through his new binoculars. Then he pointed us out to his friends, and they all sat down and looked at us through their binoculars. Rory doesn't like being looked at so he got on a rock, stood on his hind legs and waved a front leg at them, making awful grunting noises at the same time – but they wouldn't have heard that as they were too far off.

At last it was time for the hunt to start. A big fat townie shouted – 'We'll take this face due west, then swing round the shoulder to the north – remember to shoot the old birds if you can.'

(I wonder if Gorkie had heard that – he is as old as the hills and was only a rifle shot away from them!)

They all lined out on the hillside. Those at the top were puffing and blowing by the time they arrived on a knoll not very far from where we were sitting. There were two pointer dogs with keeper-hunters and about fifteen yapping spaniels and Labradors. The big fat townie shouted 'ADVANCE', and everyone started to move forward. We all watched with interest.

After about ten minutes, I saw Gorkie fly round the corner of the hill, and I saw the pointer near the top of the hill suddenly stop and lift his front leg up, sniffing as he did so. The whole line of townies stopped. About five of them with guns gathered round the pointing Pointer. They moved on slowly behind the pointing Pointer with their guns at the ready. The pointing Pointer

*... The pointing poiner sniffed and sniffed ...*

stopped again. The hunters moved on – nothing happened. The pointing Pointer sniffed and sniffed but nothing got up or ran away so the hunters let the spaniels and Labradors loose – they sniffed and hunted everywhere, but there was nothing to hunt as this was where a covey had had their grouse-baths and then moved on. Oh, the townies were angry.

'That Pointer's no good,' said the big Townie, 'I hope the one at the bottom of the hill is better.' The bottom one was a German Pointer with no tail, called 'Fritz'.

'Advance,' shouted the big townie, and they all moved forward again.

After a little while, the funniest thing happened, Henry. Fritz suddenly rushed forward, barking his head off, quickly followed by the dog at the top, and then followed by all the spaniels and Labradors that were not on leads. They were all rushing in the same direction. The townies and keeper-hunters were shouting and whistling and cursing. The big head townie couldn't run – he was too fat and unfit.

When the dogs had gone about half a rifle shot, there was a terrible noise of barking and grunting and fighting as they jumped into a peat bog where there was half a Stilton cheese. They growled at each other as they tore the cheese apart but, in the end, they shared it out and thoroughly enjoyed it. For the rest of the day, they couldn't smell a thing. They all got the most awful wopping from their masters, and were put on leads until they got home. We all grunt-laughed more than we had grunt-laughed for years and years.

The townies continued in line around the hill, and when the sun was at its highest, sat down and had a huge lunch, leaving a terrible mess of wrapping paper and tomato skins and beer cans when they had finished.

All afternoon they kept on walking but didn't see anything except for Gorkie's family of Part-Grise who had had their grouse-bath but had forgotten to move on. Gorkie was furious with them. As the townies approached, they started to get frightened and suddenly they took off.

'Shoot' – shouted the big townie.

'Don't shoot' – shouted the keeper-hunter, 'They're Partridges'.

'They're Grouse', shouted the big townies as they got further and further away.

'They're not', shouted the keeper-hunter – but they were gone by then.

Meanwhile Gorkie, who had been with his family, ran through the long heather right round the line of townies until he found a rock behind them. As soon as his family were safe, he took off, shouting his cry 'Gorback, Goback, Goback' – all the shooters turned round and twenty shots went after him but he was round the rocks by then and quite safe.

Oh, here's the baby boy Golden Eagle Post – he's going to take this all on his own today, Henry, so I hope he finds you OK. His Mum has promised him a leg of well-clawed hare when he comes home.

Be a good boy – how are you getting on with your Professor School Teacher?

Your chum

Alby

# Letter No. 26 from Alby to Henry

## (28 from Mull)

TELEPHONE
STAGLAND 303

SOMEWHERE ON THE ISLE OF MULL
ARGYLL
SCOTLAND
29th August

Hello Henry

This is a terrible time of the year – hunters everywhere and flies too. I was watching the flies buzzing around Rory the other day. He was trying to wave them away with his ears and then snapping at them. He snapped 162, and the 163rd was a wasp. He screamed with agony when it stung him on the tongue and jumped so high in the air that he hit the twig-radio bird floating overhead.

However, it is a nice warm day, and I am writing this on my lap, sitting down (rather than lying down) so that I can keep my nose in the air and pick up horrible hunter smells.

Flies made me think of Tolly Trout. All the fish in the lochs are having a bad time with the hunters just like what we are.

The other day twig-radio picked up a message which Oscar the Otter had passed on from Tolly Trout. It was all about Tolly's brother – a beautiful two-pound Brown Trout – not a Blue Trout or a White Trout but a Brown Trout.

All the trout in the lochs had been warned to be careful which flies they eat. They had been told to blow at every fly they saw before they bit it. If it went away when they blew and came back again, then it was sure to be a real one and could be eaten. If it paid no attention but just swam around in the water, then it had probably got a hook attached and was very, very dangerous.

What happened was this: Tolly's brother was looking for a good juicy blue-bottle which he could pour some Algae sauce over and have for dinner. Well, Henry, just the sort of bluebottle he was looking for settled on the water above him. It was a real beauty.

Tolly's brother couldn't resist it. He waited a moment – had a good look for a hook – couldn't see one – forgot to blow and '*bang*'. He jumped up and bit it – ooh, ooh, ooh he screamed. There was a hook. He pulled and pulled and pulled. He swam downstream and upstream and across stream and he got tireder and tireder. Then suddenly Tolly saw him and rushed up and caught him by the tail. They both pulled and pulled. The line went out and out and out and, suddenly, snap! They were free, but the fly was still caught in Tolly's brother wisdom tooth and was hurting very much; so Tolly swam him off to the Trout-world-dentist, who put Tolly's brother in his water-lily chair, pushed him backwards and looked into his mouth.

'Oh dear, oh dear,' said the trout-world-dentist, 'I'm afraid we'll never get that hook away from your wisdom tooth, and if I pull that wisdom tooth out, you will swim on one side as the wisdom tooth on the other side will make you all uneven. And if I pull both top wisdom teeth out, then you will only be able to swim upwards – so I'll have to pull all four all out.'

Tolly tried to comfort his brother. What was he going to chew those sumptuous bluebottles with? But it had to be, so Tolly held his brother down by the gills and the trout-world-dentist tied a bit of fisherman's cast onto each tooth and then he tied the other ends onto his tail, and then he told Tolly to go and get all the other trout in the pool. There were ten of them, all brown and weighing over a pound each. They each hung on to each other's tail and the trout-world-dentist hung on to the last one's tail with one end of the cast tied on to his tail and the other end on to the four wisdom teeth.

When all was ready, Tolly gurgled '1, 2, 3, 4, 6, 5' (he couldn't count very well) – then 'PULL' – and all the trout swam as hard as they could. They swam so hard that when the teeth came out, they couldn't stop and swam right on to the shore. They had to quickly wriggle back before the fisherman caught them.

Tolly's poor brother was gurgling in agony – but after he had been given a big worm to suck, he felt fine – and was quite OK next day although he knew he would have to live on soft worms and slugs for the rest of his life. This was sad because living on worms and slugs would make him lose his looks and the lady trout would no longer wink an eye as they passed him.

That was two Church-days ago, and all went well until yesterday when there was some rain, and the burns were in spate. The trouble was that Tolly's brother had become very fond of his new type of dinner and went wherever the worms and slugs were, and they were in the burns when they were in spate. But worse, Henry. When Tolly's brother lost his wisdom teeth, he obviously lost his wisdom as well, and he couldn't see any point in thinking before he bit as he didn't bite at flies any more.

Well, he was at the mouth of the burn last Church-day, gobbling up, everything that came down in spate, and he got fatter and fatter and fatter, until at last he went to sleep – and he slept, and he slept, and he slept, and the burn got bigger and bigger and bigger. Suddenly a monster worm hit him on the nose.

He woke up, didn't think, bit at the worm, and inside it, it had the biggest hook you have ever seen.

Poor old Tolly's brother. He was too tired to fight and was hauled onto the bank and netted, all in a matter of minutes.

'What a horrible looking thing,' said one townie fisherman.

'Not worth keeping,' said the other just as the first one was about to hit Tolly's brother on the head.

'Agreed,' said the first fisherman and flung Tolly's brother back in the water, where Oscar the Otter was waiting to gobble him up. That's how we heard the story – so very sad – but we do have to think what we're doing before we do it, don't we, Henry?

Old Golden Eagle Post is taking this today. I expect he'll be along quite soon.

Next week I'll tell you about a very near scrape Niall had last night – but unlike Tolly's brother, he was thinking what he was doing, so all was well.

Sleep well, Henry – I hope you can count up to ten by now.

Your old chum in the High Tops,

Alby

*... The end for Tolly Trout's brother ...*

*... A stagshot of the two of us ...*

# Letter No. 27 from Alby to Henry
## (29 from Mull)

TELEPHONE
STAGLAND 303

SOMEWHERE ON THE ISLE OF MULL
ARGYLL
SCOTLAND
5th September

Hello – Don't I look great!

Have you counted my twelve points? The last of the velvet fell off last week while I was rubbing my itchy horns on a tree in the Mossieburn – so I gave the horn a good polish and look at me now – a real REAL ROYAL. What is more, Henry, Niall has got clean horns as well, and he is a very good-looking ten pointer. I enclose a stagshot of the two of use taken by that ass Rory – he's so pleased with his six points and keeps on saying he's the best stag in Stagland, but we give him a bashing now and again, just to remind him he was only a nobber last year! He's a good boy really, Henry.

I promised to tell you about the near scrape Niall had the other day. Well, this is what happened:

We were all lying down in the afternoon sun, chewing the cud. Chewing the cud is rather difficult to explain, Henry. Roughly speaking, it's like this. We, deer, have a system you don't have. We have a sort of larder beside our tum-tums where we put the dew-grass as we eat it. Then when we have nothing better to do, we lie down and get a couple of packets of dew-grass from the larder and munch it until it is like spinach. Then we swallow it. Ask Dad – he'll make it much easier to understand! Camels do the same thing, but they have water in their humps so that they can pour watery gravy over their dew-grass after it comes out of their larder and before they chew it.

Anyway, we were all chewing the cud in the afternoon sun. The smell-sentries were out, and the sun was shining on their lovely clean horns. One or two of the nobbers were playing hide-and-seek amongst the rocks on the top of the Ben, and two of Hamish's ewes were having a gossip in the middle of the herd – all was quiet and peaceful.

Suddenly I heard a click. Niall was lying below me, and below him I saw a black thing moving about behind a rock. At first I thought it was Roger the Raven eating a myxie rabbit, then I saw a rifle barrel. Niall still hadn't noticed. It was held by a man in a bowler hat down wind of us, so the smell-sentries couldn't smell him. The rifle was pointing at Niall, Henry, he was in real danger. I didn't wait. I jumped up, ran down to Niall and kicked him on the behind – 'Run,' I grunted, 'Or you'll be sausages.'

Niall ran all right, so did the rest of the herd – way down the hill they went without stopping – past Hamish and Trash who were coming up the hill to look at their sheep; past two townies who were heating up a veal-and-ham pie on their primus stove (which was blown out by the draft created by the charging stag herd), and right down the line of horrible grouse hunters with their pointer dogs and yapping spaniels. Fritz, the German Pointer, was at the bottom and, as Rory came close, Fritz growled at him, so Rory gave a great big grunt and got Fritz fair-and-square in the face with a back-foot-kick. Poor old Fritz – he let out a yelp and was very weepy. Then the herd galloped on past Craig and up the other side of the glen – then they stopped and had a look to see what was happening.

Generally speaking, horrible hunters don't shoot 'Royals' unless some horrible hunter had paid a big cheque to get a trophy-head for above his loo-door. As it was early in the season, I thought I would be safe to let the herd go without me while I went to see what kind of hunters were out this year. So after everyone had galloped off, I turned round and walked slowly towards the bowler hat. (Dangerous thing to do, Henry, but sometimes you have to do dangerous things!)

*… I ran after them … grunting as I went …*

When I was about ten yards away, three of the funniest looking men you have ever seen got up from the heather and pointed their weapons at me. A fourth one stayed where he was – in a bog – with a machine gun. I put on my 'Royal' face and walked slowly towards them. They didn't know what to do, Henry. They had no professional hunter with them. One said 'Fire', and another said 'Don't', and another said 'He's a Royal', and another said 'He's not' – and I just walked on. Then the one lying down shouted 'He's going to trample on me', and I grunted 'You're right – get going'. They seemed to understand, Henry, because all four of them took to their feet and ran down the hill. I ran after them almost as far as the gate, grunting as I went. They were good big grunts too – helped on by my dew-grass larder door opening and shutting as I ran – and then with one last big grunt, which was almost a roar, I turned on my four heels.

I went back all the way over the hill, past the townies, past the grouse-hunters, past Fritz, past Hamish and Trash, past Craig and on up the other side to join the herd, where we all stayed until nightfall. Then we came back to the Ben. The grass beyond Craig is very nasty, Henry, it is all black and peaty.

I told Niall he really must watch out at this time of year, but he was very grateful to me for saving him from the sausage machine.

Poor old Golden Eagle Post – he's having awful trouble getting myxie rabbits and mousies – they all seem to be eaten by Roger the Raven and his chums. Roger better watch out otherwise Golden Eagle Post will wop him one and feed him to the Golden Eagle Twins.

Henry, do you remember Rory telling you about a booful young hind he met one day when he went trampies with the naughties while I was away on holiday. Well, last week he and the naughties went off to see if they could find her again. I'll tell you about that next week, Henry.

Your 'Royal' friend,

Alby

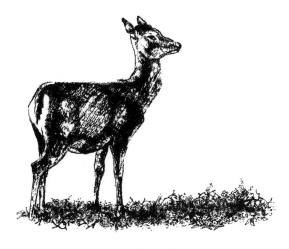

*... The booful yearling ...*

# Letter No. 28 from Alby to Henry

## (30 from Mull)

TELEPHONE
STAGLAND 303

SOMEWHERE ON THE ISLE OF MULL
ARGYLL
SCOTLAND
12 September

Henry – are you there?

We're in trouble. We can't find Rory. Have you seen him? He really is an awfully naughty boy. He never leaves his twig-radio number when he goes away.

You remember I told that he had been off on the razzle with the Naughties again, Well:

After school-time last two-days-before-Church-day, Rory said he was going on trampies with the naughties who were coming up to meet him from Bunessan. The naughties came and had mid-day-moss with us and then they trotted off with Rory down the hill.

I gather they went off in search of the hind-herds for relaxation as they thought us older stags were getting rather crotchety and bad tempered due to the approach of the mating season when everyone in Stagland gets a bit edgy, and the horrible hunters come out in force. Twig-radio says they headed off in the direction of Pennyghael and, on the way, came across Morag's hind-herd, where they called in. I was pretty sure, Henry, that Rory went off to look for that booful yearling he met when he was on trampies while I was on holiday. Well – he found her.

Apparently when they arrived at Morag's the hind herd were having their lunch all sixty of them – walking one way one moment and another way the next moment and yet another way the next moment – eating and gossiping at the same time. They all had their this-year's-babies with them, but last year's had been told to buzz off and look after themselves. Last year's babies were

*… They twee-grunted the jogging song …*

in a little bunch on one side of the herd, and Rory's booful girl was amongst them. Needless to say, this was the side of the herd where Rory and the naughties ended up.

The young hinds paid no attention to the young stags whatever, so Rory and the naughties put on an act. They licked polished their coats and their toes. They danced the horn-dance round the young hinds. They twee-grunted the Jogging Song, and they did the most beautiful stag-jog round the hinds, but all the herd did was to eat and talk. They talked and ate going north; then they ate and talked going west; then they talked and ate going south; then they ate and talked going east.

At last the staggies could bear it no longer so they made rude grunts at the young ladies and then they galloped into the middle of the herd. The hinds made a gap for them, and they just galloped out the other side, and the hinds went on eating and talking.

Rory and the naughties were desperate. They sat down in the heather and tried to think of the best thing to do. After a little while, one naughty said, 'I've got an idea', and trotted off towards the herd. The other two watched from behind the ridge. The naughty trotted right through the herd to where the young hinds were feeding. He went up to the booful one and whispered something in her ear. The booful one turned round and got the naughty an awful whack right under the jaw with her back leg. The naughty fell on the ground unconscious.

The other two were terrified. They waited until the whole herd had moved on then they went up to the unconscious nobber and licked him all over until he became conscious again.

'What did you say to her?' grunted his friend.

'I'm not going to tell you,' said the wounded naughtie, 'and I'm not going to say it to her ever again.'

'Oh dear,' said his friend, and trotted off in the direction of the herd, leaving Rory and the wounded naughtie to talk on their own.

Rory never told us what he and the wounded naughtie talked about, and twig-radio never knew. What twig-radio did know was that half-an-hour later, the fit naughtie and the booful young hind were seen trotting away from the herd together. Rory and the wounded naughtie didn't see them go but, when eventually they decided to trot past the young hinds once more on their way back to the stag herd, they noticed the booful young hind wasn't there any more, arid the fit naughtie was missing as well.

Rory was furious and said he was going to roam the hills all night looking for them, and when he found them, he was going to spear the fit naughtie into sausages with his lovely new horns. However, the wounded naughtie persuaded Rory to go back with him to the stag herd and leave the other two to themselves.

They both got back tired and sad just as the sun was setting. Rory told his Dad, Niall, all about his day chasing the booful young hind, and Niall tried to console him. The wounded naughtie said he would spend the night on the Ben, and we all went to bed.

The next morning Rory was gone. The wounded naughtie went off to look for him and twig-radio are looking as well. If Rory comes your way, Henry, please get Fred and Olly to bark very loudly so that we can hear them. The whole stag herd is very worried because it isn't safe to be alone at this time of year when the Island is full of horrible hunters.

Golden Eagle Post is with the others helping to look for Rory so I'll leave this at the myxie garage in the hopes that it will get to you somehow.

We have to find Rory – don't we, Henry?

Your old worried pal,

Alby

*... Lottie and Fergie and Lil ...*

# Letter No. 29 from Alby to Henry

## (31 from Mull)

TELEPHONE
STAGLAND 303

SOMEWHERE ON THE ISLE OF MULL
ARGYLL
SCOTLAND
19th September

Henry – All's well.

We've found Rory. King Swallow sent word back by twig-radio to say that some of his birds had seen Rory and the naughtie fighting like fury with their heads down at the bottom of the glen, near the burn. Niall and I immediately set off and eventually found both the naughties and Rory. They had all been fighting, Henry, and were covered in blood and out of breath – all because they wanted the booful year-old hind as their wife.

Niall and I did all we could to patch the wounds up and clean the blood off their coats. Then the two naughties set off home to the Bunessan Stag herd. They were like two wounded soldiers after a big battle – very sorry for themselves. We brought Rory back to the Ben. He said he was very sorry to have caused all the trouble but he really did love the year-old hind, and although he was devoted to his two old chums, the naughties, he could not stand them going off with his girl.

However, now all is forgiven, and the herd is back to normal and very much on guard against horrible hunters.

Yesterday we saw Lottie and Lil, the two Highland Ponies, for the first time this year. They are a lovely old couple – both white with shaggy mains and shaggy socks. They are used by the hunters to carry us stags off the hill to the sausage makers. They walk for miles and miles each day – very often coming home the same way as they went out all wet and cold, with no stag on their back. They are looked after by the pony boy, Fergie. He is only 17, and this is his third season already.

He has a terrible time sitting behind stones for hours and hours, waiting for a signal to bring Lottie and Lil up the hill and take whoever has been shot or perhaps just to give the 'sportsman' who has paid to shoot us, a lift up the steepest part. He is a good lad and always seems to know exactly what is happening all over the hill.

When Lottie and Lil appear we know the hunters are here in earnest – they are going to have what they call their 'cull', come what may. That means they are going to shoot enough of us to pay for the rates and to be sure there are not too many of us about for the food available – anyway, those are the reasons they give for this so called 'cull'.

Each evening Lottie and Lil are put out in a paddock just above Craig, rather than them having to walk all the way back to Torosay. Rory and some of the other stags usually go down and have a talk with them after dark – sometimes even getting a chew at their corn.

Last night Rory hobbled down to see them. They were in great form and full of news. They said the bowler hatted lot had gone, that there were two booful Dutch ladies in the Tiroran Hotel who would be coming out the next day to get their 'first stag' – but the ponies thought they would be too soft to get far up the hill. Then there were two young lads at Torosay who were very keen but got so over-excited that they couldn't keep quiet – so we might not have too much trouble from them. They also told us that there were two poachers living in a caravan not far from Pennyghael.

Just as they said that a flashlight searched the paddock and landed on Rory. There was a click, a bang, another click and another bang, but, in spite of Rory's wounds from his fight with the naughties, he had run off in time and came to no harm. Now I think he's going to stay in the herd until the break-out; his nerves are beginning to get rough and his lovely shiny coat and horns are getting rough as well.

*… A flashlight searched the paddock and landed on Rory …*

I'm afraid this letter is more about life on the hills at this time of year than exciting stories but I know you will want to know what is going on, Henry.

This week all the stags will be breaking-out, and the stags will be roaming the hills looking for hinds and fighting for them like Rory did.

Their throats will all get red and swollen as they roar and roar and roar to keep other stags away from their hinds, and they will fight, Henry, yes fight, sometimes to the death. I will be the same as the rest – it is what nature does to us at this time of year – even The Monarch will be the same. If we didn't behave like this, there would be no more dear-deer babies, and soon there would be no more deer. So forgive me, old friend, if I sign off for five or six weeks; I shall be too busy to write. I know you will be worrying about us all at this time because all the horrible hunters will be out.

I have asked Olly the Owl, who will be in charge of twig-radio, to write you a short newsletter each week from his perch on the birch trees near the Mossieburn. He is very wise and will do it very well.

Meanwhile, be good, Henry, and don't forget your old pal Alby in the mad days and nights that lie ahead. In Stagland we call this time of year 'The Rut'. I will write again in November after it is over. Meanwhile, as long as you are good, I'll be OK.

Yours ever,

Alby

# Letter No. 1 from Olly to Henry

## (32 from Mull)

TWIG-RADIO CODE
XX2

THE BIRCH TREE
MOSSIEBURN
THE ISLE OF MULL
ARGYLL
SCOTLAND
26th September

Haylo Henry –

Here is Olly Owl. I am now in charge of messages to you from us. I in charge of Twig-Radio from top of Birch Tree in Mossieburn. I have Swallow and Raven and Crow birds working de twig radios.

I now know that all stags starting to go mad chasing hinds and fighting each other and making easy shots for hunters. All stag herds are broken up and smell-sentries only done by hinds.

Ah, message just come in. Alby seen at bottom of Glen. He walking in peat-hag and roaring with big roars as he holds his big head back. No other stag wants to go near Alby when he is like this.

There was quite a big fellow came in from Bunessan last night and tried to pinch some hinds from Alby, but Alby had another roll in his peat hag, gave a big roar and charged at the Bunessan stag. There was a loud crash as they hit each other; then they both went backwards and charged again – another crash and then their horns got all tangled up. Oh, they did make a noise, grunting and roaring and scraping their horns together.

Suddenly they parted – Bunessan trotted off, and Alby started running round his hinds again rounding them up and roaring.

*… Quite a big fellow came in from Bunessan …*

A little way from Alby and his hinds, Rory and some nobbers were chewing the cud and telling each other funny stories and paying no attention.

Niall has gone off in search of some old girl friends in the south of the Island, and the rest of the Ben More stag herd are all over the place.

It is getting rather cold at nights now, Henry, and all Stagland peoples who are not deer are working on twig radio.

Last week one of the old switch-stag-policemen was sausaged. He was roaming about looking for hinds an' roaring an' rolling in the peat, but he couldn't find any hinds so he lay down in a peat hag on his own an' went to sleep with his horns sticking up over the top of the hag. He didn't realise he was very close to Alby and his friends.

The head of the horrible-keeper-hunters had a young 'guest' and was trying to find him a stag to shoot. They were walking very slowly, looking round every corner and spying all the ground they could see through their binoculars and spyglass. Suddenly they heard a stag roaring. They lay on the ground and the keeper-hunter crept up to a knoll. He saw Alby roaring at his hinds but after a long look, decided he was too splendid to shoot. Then he looked away to the right of Alby, and he saw a horn sticking up from behind a hag, and then he saw another.

The hunters crawled through wet hags and got their knees terribly black and peaty and wet. At last the keeper-hunter looked up and found he was in shooting distance of the switch-stag-policeman. He pushed the young sportsman up onto the top of a little mound from where he could see the two switch horns, then he gave him the rifle out of the case, and then they waited for the switch to stand up. They waited and waited and waited.

Suddenly Alby gave a great roar and came running over towards the switch-stag-policeman, who woke up – and got up and roared and roared and roared, and BANG – and he fell dead.

Alby and his hinds and Rory and the other nobbers all galloped off up Ben More. The keeper-hunter clapped his young guest on the back and the young guest, smiling all over, got up and thanked the keeper-hunter for getting him his first stag.

Then the keeper-hunter set fire to a bit of heather to signal Fergie to bring up Lottie and Lil to take the switch away for sausages.

Fergie wasn't long in coming, and Lottie carried the switch down the road.

The hunters went on to find other stag persons to shoot – but they never did. Alby and his hinds and Rory went back to near the top of the Ben where they spent the night, with Alby making big, big roars as the moon came up with a touch of frost on its back, and Rory making little squealy roars – just for fun!

Tweet, Tweet, Henry

From

# Olly
### Head of Twig-Radio

*… See if you can find me, Henry, I'm sitting on my branch …*

# Letter No. 2 from Olly to Henry

## (33 from Mull)

TWIG-RADIO CODE
XX2

THE BIRCH TREE
MOSSIEBURN
THE ISLE OF MULL
ARGYLL
SCOTLAND
3rd October

T woo-Twoo-Tweet, Henry

It's getting colder and colder. I hope you have got your Alby mufflers on!

Last day-after-Church-day we had quite an excitement, Henry. There was a terrible gale blowing, and it was hard to hear anything on the hill except the wind. Fergie had just put Lottie and Lil in their field at Craig for the night, after a long, wet and miserable day's stalking. Fergie pulled his bicycle out of the heather and started to push it up the road towards Torosay. As he rounded the first corner, he saw a car on the side of the road – it was a strange car – he hadn't seen it before, so he had a look round it. There didn't seem anything unusual about it, but just as he started pushing his bike again, he saw something move way up on the face of Ben More. It was getting dark but not too dark to spy.

Fergie lay down on the side of the road and, leaning against a rock, rested his spyglass on his knee. He scanned the side of the hill for a few minutes and then he saw them two men pulling a stag down the hill. He knew it wasn't the keeper-hunter or anyone connected with the estate – it must be POACHERS! The POACHERS from the Pennyghael Caravan!

Fergie hid himself in a big peat hag from where he could see what was going on. The men came closer and closer pulling their stag. It had started to rain, and the noise of the wind was terrible. They crossed the road to the car quite close to Fergie. He had never seen the men before. The stag was bundled into the boot, and the two men had an argument about whether or not to go and shoot another one.

'There is no one about,' said the first man.

'But it is cold and wet,' said the second man.

In the end they decided to just look round the corner at the foot of the Glen and, if there was nothing worth shooting, they would go back to Pennyghael for their caravan and then on to Craignure in time to catch the last ferry to Oban.

When they had gone, Fergie got out his knife and, after he had opened the boot of the car, he made a hole in the bottom of the boot. Then he turned the stag over so that the blood dripped through the hole on to the road.

After shutting the boot, Fergie went down to Craig and knocked at the door. Your friends, who had rented Craig, were very nice to Fergie and gave him what he asked for – a bag of sugar. Fergie went back to the car, opened the petrol tank and tipped the sugar into the tank. Then he closed the tank again, got hold of his bicycle and made off up the road. (You see, Henry, if you put sugar in a petrol tank, the engine will stop a short time after it has been started).

Fergie pushed and pedalled, pushed and pedalled as hard as he could. He wanted to get to a telephone to tell Constable Donald about the poachers before they got back to the car.

Fergie saw car lights behind him. The car passed him. It was the poachers' car. Suddenly it spluttered and stopped. Fergie didn't know whether to get off his bike or not – but he didn't – he biked on past the car. Both men got out at once saying nasty things. They called to Fergie to help them. Fergie went on bicycling but it was tough going up the hill so he had to get off and walk. The first man ran after him. Fergie started running too the faster he ran, the faster the first man ran. But the first man was too fast for Fergie and caught him.

'You give me that', said the first man, pulling the bike away from Fergie. 'You walk home. I'm going to get some help to mend my car – we have an important package in it.'

At that moment the second man saw the blood trickling out of the boot.

'Look at this,' he shouted.

The first man dragged Fergie and his bike back to the car. The two men opened the boot and saw a hole in it.

'Did you do this,' asked the first man, shaking Fergie by the neck.

'No – no – Sir,' said Fergie.

'Then who did?' asked the first man.

'You must have made the hole with the stag's horn as you put the stag in,' said Fergie. 'That would be impossible,' said the second man. 'The horns would break.' He shook Fergie again.

A car's headlights came round the corner. Fergie managed to break away from his captor and waved his hands up and down in the middle of the road. The car stopped, and two nice young ladies asked if they could help. The first man asked if they could get a mechanic to mend their car. He didn't see Fergie pointing to the blood on the road which was visible in the headlights as it leaked through the poachers' car boot. Nor did he see the young lady driver winking at him in return. The lady driver told the poacher she would find a mechanic, gave a toot and drove on.

Fergie was terrified being left alone with those two horrid men until help came. He had a brainwave.

'Let's go down to Craig and ask the nice people there if we can have shelter and a cup of tea,' he said.

'Good idea,' said the first man, 'but no funny business mind.'

'Oh, no funny business,' said Fergie.

So down they went, knocked on the door, and when the people at Craig saw who it was, they immediately invited all three of them to come in. They offered them tea but they said they were sorry that they had run out sugar!

After half an hour or so, car headlights appeared again. Two lots of them. The cars stopped by the poachers' car. The two men and Fergie thanked the tenants for their tea and went up the bank to the road. What do you think, Henry?

It was Constable Donald, with the head-horrible-keeper-hunter and the two nice young ladies in the car.

As soon as the poachers saw who was there, they cursed Fergie and said they would 'get him for this' and ran down the hill. It was no use – the Constable and the keeper were too fast for them. They caught up with them, grabbed them by the legs in a rugger tackle and pulled them to the ground. They were in handcuffs in no time at all.

Fergie showed the Constable the stag and told him his story. The poachers went back to Oban on the last ferry all right, but without their stag or caravan. They went back as poachers-prisoners. The two nice young ladies took Fergie and his bicycle home.

I hope these are getting through OK Henry. Golden Eagle Post is getting awfully fat these days. He must be picking up the no-use-for-sausages bits of the sausaged stags and devouring them in large quantities.

More next week.

Tweet, Tweet,

*… The stags were roaring so loudly that …*

# Letter No. 3 from Olly to Henry

## (34 from Mull)

TWIG-RADIO CODE
XX2

THE BIRCH TREE
MOSSIEBURN
THE ISLE OF MULL
ARGYLL
SCOTLAND
10th October

Tweet-a-woo, Tweet-a-woo, Henry.

It is getting cold at night, and the stags are roaring so loudly that nobody can get any sleep.

Henry, have you tried roaring like the stags yet? Try now – get down on all four legs like Alby. Now hold your head up AND ROAR. Now croak a bit like a frog and make the croaks longer-and-longer-and-longer until they become a R-O-A-R. Now, Henry, go on ROARING until your roars get so deep they sound like the bottom note of the piano …

Ah, here's a message coming through from Swallow three, by way of Swallow one and Raven six. I'll tell you what it says, Henry.

It's all about Niall. He's been in trouble with the Bunessan herd. It seems that he went down to the Bunessan hind herd where he had got some ladies last year and thought he might do the same again. When he arrived he couldn't see any stag with them. No one was roaring, and there were no horns to be seen so he lick-polished himself and started prancing round the herd, making eyes at the ladies. Then he let out a little croaking roar – well, do you know Henry?

The biggest animal you have ever seen came out of a peat hag. He was ji-normous and had a roar like an elephant but he had no horns. He advanced on Niall who looked at him slobbering from the mouth. (He was a hummel, Henry. That is a stag with no horns but usually very big with a thick head and very fierce.) Niall went mad when he saw him. He put his head down and CHARGED. He got the hummel right in the middle of the head. They met with an almighty CRASH, and the hummel's head was so solid that poor Niall broke the top off one of his horns and fell over from the shock.

*… He was just about to butt him one in the tummy when …*

The hummel looked at the figure of Niall lying on the ground and gave him a nasty kick. Then he was just about to butt him one in the tummy when two small stags came rushing through the hinds from different directions, and bashed the hummel on each side of his body and then ran for it.

These were the 'naughties' of Bunessan, Henry. They were talking to some school chums a little way off, but had recognised Niall as the Dad of their great friend Rory so had come to help.

The hummel was furious. He didn't know whether to chase the naughties or stamp on Niall. Just then, there was a BANG and the hummel fell dead.

Niall got up, shook himself and ran just as another shot rang out. It scraped the top of his back. He and the naughties and the naughties' friends and the hinds ran and ran and ran until they were on the other side of the burn.

The hummel had been shot by one of the booful ladies living in the hotel, who was very upset she had got her feet wet and her new plus-fours had peat on them and worse – she never noticed that the stag she had shot had no horns – so there would be nothing to put over her silken boudoir door for her boyfriends to see. That was why she had fired the other shot in the hopes of getting Niall in spite of the keeper-hunter telling her not to.

The keeper-hunter was very pleased because he doesn't like hummels, and as it was the beautiful lady's first – yes, Henry – YES, HENRY – she had blood splashed all over her beautiful face! – and WAS SHE ANGRY?! She said she would never go stalking again and tramped off down the hill on her own – so that was that!

I have just heard from brother-owl, who is watching Professor Red Deer and his schoolroom over in Mossieburn. He says that Professor Red Deer told him today that twenty seven stags have so far been sausaged this year, and his stagputor reckons the horrible hunters will be looking for the same again – so we all have to watch out, during the last two weeks of the season, Henry.

Alby is now with the Ben More hinds. Rory and his chums are not far away from him. Niall has got all the Bunessan hinds with the naughties and their chums not far from Bunessan. Niall is sorry about his horn – although it is only the tip of one of his points that he has lost.

Tweet, tweet, Henry. Golden Eagle Post is getting very difficult – says he only picks up mail from Alby or senior stags. I told him I would report him to the Posteagle General on Ben Nevis if he didn't watch out, and then he would lose his twig-radio licence – that made him think – I think!

On behalf of Alby,

Yours,

Olly.

*… A stagshot of the booful lady's blooded face on Fergie's mantlepiece…*

*… Fergie gave him a big wave as he passed …*

# Letter No. 4 from Olly to Henry

## (35 from Mull)

TWIG-RADIO CODE
XX2

THE BIRCH TREE
MOSSIEBURN
THE ISLE OF MULL
ARGYLL
SCOTLAND
*17th October*

T woo-Tweet Henry,

It's so wild and windy now that the birds are finding it hard to hold the twigs in their beaks so it is sometimes difficult to pick up their messages correctly.

This week most of the swallows have been watching Alby – poor old boy – he's had a difficult time. He's getting very thin, and his throat must be hurting him a great deal with all the roaring he has been doing. When stags get like this, Henry, they don't eat for days on end – just wallow in peat hags and roar and roar and roar and chase their hinds and get madder and madder.

On the day after Church-day (not many stags go to church at this time of year, Henry. Professor Red Deer does have services in the Mossieburn but only very few stags attend – one or two very old ones who live in the brackeny woods, one or two young ones and one or two who have been wounded by the horrible hunters.)

Anyway, as I was saying. On the day after Church-day soon, after dawn, Alby walked away from his hinds on Ben More – just walked away, Henry, for no reason. It was a beautiful day, and twig-radio operators could see Alby quite clearly as he walked off, slightly unsteady on his legs. Every now and again he would trot a little then he would stand and roar at nothing for no known reason. Then he would lie down for a bit and then move on again. His neck is very thick and the long hairs covering it are black and tangled with peat. His tummy is empty and his body looks all hunched, up. His eyes are droopy and his tongue is hanging out most of the time. Like all the other stags on the Island, Henry, he doesn't know what he is doing or where he is going – or why. In fact, he was going in the general direction of Laggan Forest.

About midday he passed quite close to Fergie and the two ponies. Fergie had been watching him all morning and gave him a wave as he passed but Alby never noticed, nor did he see the hunters who had been close to him earlier – they had taken no notice of him because he was a Royal and in such poor condition.

It was evening-moss-time when Alby got to Laggan, but he didn't feel like evening moss, he just wanted to wallow some more in a peat hag and roar, so this is what he did until nightfall when he went to sleep.

\* \* \* \* \* \* \* \* \* \* \* \* \* \* \* \* \* \* \* \* \* \* \* \* \* \* \* \* \* \* \* \* \* \* \* \* \*

Meanwhile Rory had taken over the Ben More hinds in the absence of his Grandpa, and Rory felt very grown-up and strutted round the hinds every five minutes, uttering short sharp squeaky roars as he went. He tried to get peat on his coat to make him look grownup, but it wouldn't stick to him because his coat was too shiny.

In. the middle of the afternoon another young stag – younger than Rory – thought he should have the hinds for a bit so he suddenly let out a puny sort of roar and charged Rory, who saw him coming and stepped aside. The attacker tripped on a bit of peat and went head over heels onto the wet hag, grunting as he went. Rory just grunt-giggled at the sight of his assailant lying upside down in the peat hag – but he didn't grunt-giggle for long – because over the hill came the biggest switch you have ever seen, with evil eyes and sharp switch points.

He gave an almighty roar and trotted towards Rory with his tongue hanging out. Rory gave a challenging little grunt-roar and then he saw the switch's face. He knew he would be skewered if he stayed so he went very fast indeed – right over the top of Ben More and down into the Mossieburn, hotly followed by the young stag who had attacked him, and that is where they are now as far as I know.

\* \* \* \* \* \* \* \* \* \* \* \* \* \* \* \* \* \* \* \* \* \* \* \* \* \* \* \* \* \* \* \* \* \* \* \* \*

When dawn came, Alby gave a little roar, stood up and stretched himself. He couldn't think where he was but immediately started walking up wind, roaring and wallowing in the hags as he went. Suddenly he stopped. He thought he heard a roar in the distance and he smelt hinds. He let out the most almighty roar and trotted in the direction his smell-nose led him.

Alby was just coming up to a big rock when he stopped to scrape his horns in a big hag. He lifted his head up and was about to give a mighty roar of challenge but, before he could do so, another stag roared from behind the rock. Alby trotted round the rock and there, facing him was the biggest stag you have ever seen.

They both put their heads back and roared and roared. Then they started to walk round in circles, pawing the ground as they went and roaring – roaring – roaring. Then suddenly, Alby put

*… He roared and galloped right up to the stag …*

his head down and charged the big stag. Bang – crash – grunt scream – grunt. Then they broke loose and the big stag vanished over the ridge with Alby in pursuit.

When he got to the top of the ridge, Alby saw the hinds and the big stag with them. This was too much for him. He roared and galloped right up to the big stag, who didn't see him coming. Alby put his head down – all the hinds scattered and the big stag got number ten and eleven point right through his side. He screamed in pain and hobbled off. Alby followed and got him another stab in the hindquarters. The big stag moved faster and, when he was out of sight and away from the hinds, Alby returned and took charge of them.

For the next two days Alby had possession of the Laggan hinds and no one troubled him.

The big stag stumbled on until he came to the foot of a deep Corrie where he lay down and licked his wounds and slept. He was in Parliament Corrie, Henry, and the Big Stag was The Monarch – but Alby didn't know that.

Tweet-Tweet, Henry – wrap up in your woollies – the snow will soon be here. I'll have to give some anti-freeze to the twig-radio operators.

Alby's chum

Olly

*… Bellowing away with a hind under each horn …*

# Letter No. 5 from Olly to Henry

## (36 from Mull)

TWIG-RADIO CODE
XX2

THE BIRCH TREE
MOSSIEBURN
THE ISLE OF MULL
ARGYLL
SCOTLAND
24th October

T wit-a-roaring-woo, Henry.

What a noisy time of year this is! Frosty evenings making the stags' roars sound so clear and challenging.

King Swallow twigged back a message the other night saying that Alby was a wonderful sight standing on a rock silhouetted against the moon and bellowing away with a hind under each horn. Stagland can be cruel yet wonderful, full of hate, yet full of love; full of sadness, yet full of joy – rather like your own world, Henry – I wouldn't wonder.

Anyway, Alby is still wallowing round the Laggan hind herd, Niall is still at Bunessan, that nasty switch is still with the Ben More hind herd, while Rory and chum were with us in the Mossieburn, but we had a little excitement two days after church-day.

Rory and his chum decided they were going to go and have a news with the hind smell-sentries at the top of Ben More and see how that big switch was behaving. They crept up behind some rocks out of sight of the herd in case the switch should see them and make a charge. When they got to the rock nearest the top hind smell-sentry, Rory put his head over the rock to see where the switch was and, do you know, Henry, as he did so, two big switch horns appeared not far from the other side of the rock. It was the switch himself only a short gun shot away. He came closer and closer and closer. Rory was terrified so he lay down behind the rock and tried to look dead.

His chum scampered off down the hill into the birch-wood. The switch gave a roar and chased the friend for a little way. Then he turned round to come back and saw Rory lying behind the rock. Rory was breathing so fast that his turn-turn was going up and down like a pair of bellows, and he didn't look the least bit dead.

The switch prodded Rory's turn with awful big prods, and each time he did so, Rory gave a little grunt.

'Ah, ha,' thought the switch as he walked back half a rifle shot. Then he put head down and CHARGED. Rory jumped to his feet and ran off down the hill. The switch had his head down and never saw Rory scamper off – on he charged – on – on until CRASH.

He hit his switch horns against the rock Rory had been hiding behind. He knocked himself senseless, Henry, and fell down just where Rory had been lying. The crash was so loud that all the hinds scampered.

*… A party of horrible hunters … were only two rifle shots away …*

As it so happened, a party of horrible hunters had been hunting the switch and were only two rifle shots away. They had seen the whole episode and were astonished. Slowly they crawled through the bracken to the switch. There was no need to shoot him – he had knocked himself so hard that he was already dead – so the head-keeper-hunter took away the switch's non-sausage material, made a little bonfire to attract Fergie's attention and, in due course, Lottie carried the switch off for sausages.

Rory saw the switch being carried down the hill. He knew all the big stags were getting very tired, and he knew the hunting season for stags finished the next day, so he licked-polished himself all over, trotted up the hill, round the corner, down into the burn and up the other side, and there he found the Ben More hinds, including his own Mum, Morag. He looked very cute and exciting to the hinds after all those big rough noisy. weary stags had been chasing them around and round for almost three weeks, and they were very pleased to see him.

Rory felt very important, and he tried to give one of his little squeaky roars, but it didn't come out that way, Henry – it came out as a huge great ROAR, like his Dad, Niall's, and like his Granddad Alby's. He was a real grown-up stag now, and we are all sure he will stay with the Ben More hinds until the end of the marrying season, and perhaps go back to them next year as a fine eight-pointer.

Meanwhile, Henry, the twig radio is being run almost entirely by King Swallow's team now as Roger the Raven and Harold the Hoodie and all the other Stagland birds with dirty habits are too full and bloated from gobbling up non-sausage bits of stag that they have found lying about the hill. The trouble is that before I write again, I'm afraid the Swallow team will have left for the warm lands in the far South as it is getting too cold for them to swallow up here. What's more, I don't think Alby will be back in Mossieburn for another two to three weeks so we'll just have to do the best we can with the help of the few twig operators left and the ear-shaking-team on the ground, like Bunnie and Ronnie and their hare friends. But we'll manage somehow.

Golden Eagle Post and his family are just about as bloated as our other bloated friends – so I may have to bring my next week's letter myself. As you know, I can only see in the dark, so I can only come by night otherwise I could not read the signposts. Tell Fred that if he sees two headlights gliding at midnight, not to bark as it will only be me.

Your wise old bird,

$Olly$

P. S. I will tweet before I glide in, then Fred will know who it is.

*… Olly upside down after his long flight to your home.*
*He is talking to Bit and Bat who always hang upside down …*

# Letter No. 6 from Olly to Henry

## (37 from Mull)

TWIG-RADIO CODE
XX2

THE BIRCH TREE
MOSSIEBURN
THE ISLE OF MULL
ARGYLL
SCOTLAND
31st October

Twoo-eet, Henry,

Twig radio is very short-handed now. The Swallow team have gone, and the Stagland birds of prey have overeaten – never mind – here's the news.

Firstly, I got to your house OK last week but, as I was flying over Crianlarich, a flying jumbo flew over me with such speed that I got caught in its vapour trail and found myself doing 500 miles per hour instead of twenty, with the result that when I got to your home, my undercarriage had got all frozen up and wouldn't let down so I had to land on my beak and rest on the branch above Fred's kennel, hanging on like a bat. My headlights were still shining as the switch in my brain had frozen up like my undercarriage!

However, when the dawn came, and the sun came over the horizon, the temperature rose, my undercarriage unfroze, my lights went off, and I fell – plop – from the branch right on top of a juicy mousie for breakfast – ooh, it was good. I did have to switch on my headlights again for a moment to see what it was I was eating!

When I got back here, my new-born tweeting baby owl gave me a message from Ronnie the Roe, to say that the big stags were now so tried that they were all lying about in peat hags on their own, while their sons and grandsons were having fun with the rather weary herds of hinds.

Freddie the Fox saw Alby the other day. he was looking very tired and weary, lying in a peat hag all on his own, about two rifle shots away from the Laggan lot. Freddie said 'Boom Boom' to Alby, but Alby only looked up and told him to take his boom-booms somewhere else. Poor old Boy – he can hardly even roar now.

I hear that Rory is still with the Ben More girls, a stranger is with the Laggan lot and one naughtie is with the Bunessan bunch with ten very booful young ladies, including Rory's old girl friend. Both naughties are roaring little roars now but neither has managed the grown-up deep base roar like Rory has.

Now it is after the end of the stag shooting season, the horrible hunters have gone back to their office desks to make enough money to come hunting again next year, while the horrible-keeper-hunters, with the help of Fergie and his two ponies, come to the hill each day to sausage

*… They either have to sausage the baby as well or leave it to the mercies of Freddie the Fox …*

a hind or two. This is rather a worry because sometimes they sausage a hind with a baby, and either have to sausage the baby as well or leave it to the mercies of Freddie the Fox and his chums.

No one seems to know where the Monarch has got to. He hasn't been seen since he went back to the deep Corrie at Laggan to nurse his wounds – but we don't worry too much about him as he has got the Lord-Chamber-Lain to look after him – that is always assuming the Lord-Stag-Chamber-Lain hasn't got sausaged himself.

Usually at this time of year, when we don't really know who is alive and who is dead, we arrange a count across the stag herds of the Island. The easiest way to do this, Henry, is through Hamish and Trash when they gather their sheep in for the sales. This is due to happen after next Church-day, and Professor Red Deer is getting out his bracken-papers and birch twig pencil so that he can record the reports as they come in.

All the leaves are falling off the trees now, and it's getting very, very cold. The young stags have started school again, and most wear heather mufflers round their horns. Gorkie the Grouse has gone all black and spends his time sitting on a stone shouting nasty shouts at anyone who comes near him. Ronnie the Roe is OK but the horrible hunters are bagging one or two Roe Does for chipolatta sausages (wee sausages that taste a bit better than the big ones!) Otherwise, with the Townies away, and the love-making over for another year, we are all well, if weary – and those who sleep in the dark are getting longer sleeps, while those, like me, who sleep in the day, are getting shorter sleeps.

Next week we'll let you know how Hamish and Trash get on with the sheeping gathering and the stag count.

Golden Eagle thinks he can manage this one, Henry.

Tweet-a-woo for now,

Olly

# Letter No. 1 *from the Professor*

## (38 *from Mull*)

TELEPHONE:
STAGLAND 333

BOY'S SCHOOL
TUFTED-TOP-TREE
MOSSIEBURN
THE ISLE OF MULL
7th November

Good morning, Henry

This is the Professor. You will notice that I am wearing my Professor's Garland.

I'm afraid that Olly was so tired after going Jumbo-speed to your house that he has had to go for a holiday to the roof of the Abbey in Iona – so I'm going to try to keep you in touch until Alby comes back in about two weeks time.

Olly told you that Hamish and Trash and the other shepherds would-be gathering their sheep this week and trying to find out which stag-persons had been sausaged while the horrible hunters were up.

Well, on the day after Church-day we watched Mr MacTavish and Hamish and Trash start gathering from just above your house at Craig. (You will remember, Henry, that Mr MacTavish is the farmer here, Hamish the shepherd and Trash his collie dog.) They scoured the hills for almost three hours, herding all the sheep down to the road and talking to the deer when they met them.

Hamish found one poor nobber who had got a bullet in his shoulder from one ignorant hunter, or more likely a poacher. He put some heather-wine in the wound and told the nobber to go back to the herd and stop grunting.

Then Mr MacTavish found a hind with a broken leg and her calf still with her. He took great trouble to make a splint out of his walking stick and strap it on with bandages. The hind came to see me and I put her in bed in Mossiospital for a few days. I'm sure she'll come all right. Her little stag calf stayed with her and he will be company for her.

Trash talked to many of the sheep about the hunting season, and they all had stories about how they had helped to confuse the horrible hunters. Some of the sheep knew where the shepherds could find wounded stags, and slowly we gathered them in to the Mossiospital. I think all the ones we have got will get better by the next new-grass time.

There was a mysterious moment though, Henry. The shepherds were down near Laggan and were gathering in their sheep. It was a lovely day, and all was going well until suddenly Trash disappeared. Mr MacTavish and Hamish whistled and whistled and nothing happened. Hamish thought he knew where Alby was resting and thought Trash might have gone there. He went to look and found Alby but no Trash. Alby was quite well but still looked very tired, and said he had heard Trash wuffing earlier in the day but had never see him.

Hamish was very worried and called all the other dogs in – but no one had seen Trash for almost two hours. The shepherds gave up gathering the sheep and combed the hill, whistling and calling for Trash. Alby tried to help by struggling out of his peat hag and sort of croak-roaring in the hopes that his old friend Trash would hear him, but nothing happened.

Eventually Hamish burst into tears and said they must go home as it was getting dark – maybe Trash would appear in the morning, but he was afraid he had eaten some poison or got caught in a trap or had a heart attack or something – Trash was fifteen (or in your terms 120 years old).

After the sun had gone down, all the shepherds came to Mossieburn to tell us what they had found out about the number of sausaged deer and wounded deer.

Mr MacTavish said they had heard of sixty-two stags being sausaged and four more were in Mossiospital.

*... I told him to run after his master ...*

Hamish said he had heard of six hinds and seven roe-does being sausaged and only the one with the broken leg in Mossiospital.

I put all these figures on the Stagputor and wished our friends 'Goodnight' – poor Hamish was very worried about Trash.

As they all went off down the Ben, there was a funny sort of scraping noise in the heather. I couldn't think what it was – so went to look. It was Trash pulling himself along on his tummy.

I asked him what he was doing, Henry. He said he was so ashamed of himself disappearing for so long that he was shy of seeing his master again. He told me he had been doing something 'very important' but wouldn't say what it was.

I told him to run after his master and say he was sorry, then ask his permission to come back and see me and tell me his story. He ran off and an hour later he came back. I'll tell you what he told me in my next letter, Henry – but you must keep it a secret.

Ah, here's one of the Eaglets representing Golden Eagle Post – I hope he'll take this one.

Yours very sincerely,

## Professor Red Deer

*... By the tufted-top-tree ...*

# Letter No. 2 from the Professor

## (39 from Mull)

TELEPHONE:
STAGLAND 333

BOYS' SCHOOL
TUFTED-TOP-TREE
MOSSIEBURN
THE ISLE OF MULL
15th November

I hope you slept well, Henry.

This is the Professor.

In my last letter I told you I would let you know where Trash had been when Hamish lost him, on condition that you didn't tell anyone.

This is what happened:

Trash was rounding up about thirty ewes and lambs on the Laggan hills, and he intended to bring them back to the road just North of Craig. He wasn't going very fast as he was well ahead of the others and already out of sight of his master, Hamish.

As he traversed back and forward, but always keeping his sheep going down the hill, he smelt 'stag', The smell got closer and closer. Then behind a big hag, he saw two big horns.

Trash let the sheep wander and crept up to the stag. He was very ill, Henry, with a very big head and a sad thin body. The stag and Trash looked at each other for some moments. Then Trash realised he was looking at The Monarch himself.

Trash went closer, then stood on his hind legs and saluted with his paw. The old Monarch lifted his foreleg in acknowledgement and beckoned Trash to come closer.

'Trash old friend,' he said 'I'm old and badly wounded in a stag fight. Several horrible hunters have come by me, but all have said they hoped I would get better so that I can breed some more

*… He beckoned Trash to come closer …*

big heads – but I won't, Trash – I just know I won't, and I don't think I want to now – I would sooner go and join the flying Jumbos because I am old and tired.'

Trash went close to the old stag and snuggled in under his neck.

'Don't be like that,' said Trash. 'You are The Monarch of all stag-herds on the Island, and they all love you.' But The Monarch was clear that he wanted to join the Flying Jumbos.

'When I climb up into their vapour trails like what Professor Red Deer said Stag Jesus did,' grunted The Monarch, 'I want you, Trash, to tell all Stagland that I have gone to join the dear deer-God, and I want you to tell them I love them all very much – not just the stags and hinds, but Olly and Ronnie and Roger and Gorkie, and everyone on this lovely land – yes, even Freddie the Fox, and tell them, Trash, not to hate the horrible hunters – we have to be "thinned-out" every now and again so that there is enough food for our babies – and babies are very important to all of us. Just like what they are in Henry's world.'

The Monarch went on talking like this for nearly two hours while Trash went round licking The Monarch's wounds and trying to make him more comfortable.

'Where is the Lord-Stag-Chamber-Lain?' asked Trash.

'I don't know,' said The Monarch, 'he has passed by several times, looking for me, but I don't want him to see me looking like this – it will only worry him, and he has his own matters to look after. When I leave, he will have to know – someone will tell him where my remains are to be found, and then, Trash will have to go to the Professor and find out who beat me in battle. And if he is a strong Royal Stag like me, he will have to be proclaimed Monarch.'

The Monarch got very tired and the light was fading.

'You better go now, dear Trash,' said The Monarch. 'Say nothing to anyone except the

Professor – but come back here sometime around stag-Christmas time. I expect you will find my lovely horns and bits of hair but, by that time, I will be with the flying Jumbos – and then you can tell the Professor to tell the Lord-Stag-Chamber-Lain to find the next Monarch.'

There were big tears in Trash's eyes as he licked The Monarch goodbye first on his big horns and then on his nose. And there were tears in The Monarch's eyes as he gave Trash a little kick with his foreleg.

Trash stood on his hind legs and saluted with his front paw – his very best and smartest salute, it was. The Monarch raised his right foreleg for a moment and then went to sleep.

Trash galloped off into the dark towards Ben More, to see the Professor – you know the rest, Henry.

I'm afraid this is a very sad letter. The other baby eaglet said he would take it – I hope Alby will be back in the Mossieburn by next week. Don't tell anyone about Trash and The Monarch just yet.

Be good and do your homework well, Henry. You must come to my school one day.

Yours sincerely,

# Professor Red Deer

*… I'm back again at the Mossieburn …*

# Letter No. 30 from Alby to Henry

## (40 from Mull)

TELEPHONE:
STAGLAND 303

SOMEWHERE ON THE ISLE OF MULL
ARGYLL
SCOTLAND
21st November

Hello Henry,

I'm back again – but only just! I walked all the way over from Laggan last night and felt very tired indeed by the time I got to the Mossieburn. Before the marrying time I could do the journey in an hour and feel fine after it – but the marrying season takes a lot out of us, Henry, and the journey last night took all of three hours. It is so cold too, none of us has eaten for two or three weeks so we are all very thin.

All the herd stags have come back to Mossieburn from their hind herds now – that is except those who were sausaged. We have made our winter home a little higher than last year, as the grass seems better up here.

Niall and Rory both came back last night. Neither of them is any the worse from the hunting season. Niall has asked Rory to look after the smell-sentries until he is stronger, and Rory has asked some of the other young stags to help him. This should be all right, Henry, as Rory will take the job very seriously, and not too many people are interested in us at this time of year anyway.

I'll tell you one thing that has been worrying me, Henry.

On the last night that I rested in my peat hag at Laggan, I seemed to remember charging a big booful stag the week before. I thought I had stabbed him with my top points because they hurt a little, but I couldn't remember any details. And then I thought I remembered taking over the big stag's hinds for a bit, but, I couldn't remember what had happened to the big stag. You see, Henry, we big stags oughtn't really to fight with other big stags as it gives a bad example to the rest of the herd, but sometimes, when the rut is going full blast, we forget what we are doing.

Anyway, I thought I had better go and tell The Monarch about my fight, as he likes to know what befalls the most booful stags in the forest at love-making time, so I went to the deep Corrie at Laggan Forest.

There was no stag-person to be seen for a little while, and then I saw two or three stags coming up from the burn. The leader was my friend Chamber-Lain. When he was about two shots away, I walked over to join him. He was nearly as tired as I was Henry, and so were his two chums.

Anyway, I said I wanted to see The Monarch to tell him that I thought I had skewered one of the big stags of the forest and hadn't seen him since.

The Chamber-Lain said he had been looking for The Monarch for days but couldn't find him. He said he was sure he hadn't been sausaged as the Twig Radio would have reported it if he had.

We both wondered very hard where The Monarch could be. Chamber-Lain said he would pass on my message next time he saw him – so I set off for home.

*… We stopped to have a blether …*

As I was coming down to the little Loch to the South of Ben Buie, who should I meet but Hamish and Trash. We stopped to have a blether, and I mentioned the fact that I had been looking for The Monarch but that no one seemed to know where he was. Trash put his ears up and then crept off into some long heather with his tail between his legs.

'What's wrong with you?' said Hamish – but Trash just lay quiet and wouldn't woof at all. We both knew that Trash had something to woof about – but we also knew, by the look on his face, that, whatever it was, was his secret.

When I got back here, Henry, I was gossiping to the Professor and told him the story of Trash. 'Trash is a fine fellow,' grunted the Professor.

He told me that Trash had got a secret which he had promised not to share with anyone except the Professor, and he was just keeping his promise. So there was nothing I could do Henry.

Now I don't know what Trash's secret was, and I don't know where The Monarch is – but I do wonder if Trash does, and I do just wonder if that is Trash's secret. I may never know the answer to either because Trash is a good faithful woofer.

Meanwhile I hope all goes well with you, Henry, and that you are working hard with your Professor. I am sorry I went crazy for four or five weeks but that is the law of nature.

I shall now be able to keep you in touch as we start to plough our way through the cold, cold winter.

We have one bit of good news. Golden Eagle Post has now got four full-time Golden-Eagle-Post-Persons; Golden Eagle Post himself, his wife and the two eaglets – so they should always be on time.

Did you try roaring, Henry? Give me a big 'Hello' and then a roar. If I can hear you, I'll roar back. On second thoughts, I don't think I will as my throat is too sore from roaring these last weeks.

Until next week, Henry – be a good boy and look after Dad and Mum.

Your old friend, who is glad to be back

Alby

*… Henry trying to roar …*

# Letter No. 31 from Alby to Henry

## (No 41 from Mull)

TELEPHONE:
STAGLAND 303

SOMEWHERE ON THE ISLE OF MULL
ARGYLL
SCOTLAND
28th November 1985

Hello Henry,

You know, Henry, I didn't really hear you roar last week – please try again when you get this letter. Go outside – look to the west. Take a deep breath. Hold your head back and ROAR and ROAR and ROAR, I'll let you know if I heard you in my next.

Rory says he will be listening as well.

This week has been taken up with trying to help the hind herd escape from the hunters. We had the head-horrible-keeper-hunter up here with a chum, plus Fergie and his two ponies, last week, and they chased those wretched hinds round and round the hill, sausaging one every now and again.

Rory and two of his new nobber friends, who left the hind herd when the marrying season started, went out on a sort of patrol. They walked about at the bottom of the hill below the hind herd and, as soon as they saw the hunters, Rory waved his lovely eight points from side to side so that the nearest twig-radio-bird could see them. Twig Radio then flew to just above the head of the hind herd and waved his twig from side to side. Then the hinds knew there was danger coming up the hills.

The trouble is that the hind herds are always gossip-munching and never really pay attention. When one of their smell-sentries does smell danger, they all get up and do a little dance to the right and then a dance to the left. Then they lick-polish their babies. Then they argue about which way to go, and eventually, after about half a dozen of them have been sausaged, they all take off at high speed – usually in the wrong direction so they have to gallop for miles before they are safe enough to munch-gossip again.

I believe eight hinds were sausaged, and the nobbers nearly got into trouble as well because they mobbed the keeper-hunter thinking they were safe as stag shooting had finished. But they didn't realise, Henry, that a nobber with his nobs cut off looks very like a hind, and the keeper-hunters think nothing of sausaging a nobber if he gets in the way – well:

Rory and his nobbers had done all they could to help save, the hinds but they hadn't been very successful so the nobbers thought they would get their own back on the hunter.

While he was taking the bit-of-no-good-for-sausages away from one of the sausaged hinds, the keeper-hunter had taken his coat off and laid it on a tuft of heather. One of the nobbers crept

*... The keeper-hunter had taken his coat off ...*

up to it very slowly, while the keeper-hunter wasn't looking, pushed the jacket into a peaty puddle and JUMPED on it, making such a splash the keeper-hunter looked round and saw what had happened. He was so angry that he ran to where his rifle was to teach the nobber a lesson – but his rifle wasn't where he had laid it. Do you know why, Henry? Because the other nobber had crept up, put his nobs through the sling and trotted off down the hill with the rifle dangling from side to side.

Well, you should have seen the hunter. He was FURIOUS, Henry, and shouted all sorts of nasty words at the nobbers, telling them that they would both be sausages before nightfall.

Rory, who was watching from a rock, grunt-laughed so much that the hunter started shouting at him as well, but Rory came up close to the hunter and grunted that the nobbers were only having a bit of fun and didn't really mean any harm. Then he did a little stag-jog round the hunter, grunting the jogging song. This made the hunter feel much better and, after a little while, the nobber came back with the rifle, and then both nobbers hung the hunter's coat on Rory's horns and blew and blew and blew until it was dry. Then all three lick-polished the rifle and the coat and put them back where they had found them. After kneeling down on their front legs and wagging their tails in salute, all three jogged off down the hill, leaving the keeper-hunter feeling as though he was a very important person, which made him feel a very happy man.

Good manners help any awkward situation, Henry.

I meant to tell you in my last that Rory is now head Prefect in Professor Red Deer's school, Henry. He does a lot to help the new nobber-pupils and is a very proud eight-pointer-stag-prefect-person.

Oh dear, baby eaglet says his Dad is all overeaten on non-sausage-hind-material so he'll have to take this himself. The trouble with the eaglets taking the post is that they drop in at every village on the way to watch the animal-icket matches on the Green.

Be good, Henry, work hard, play hard, laugh hard and, Henry, ROAR hard.

Your old ally,

Alby

# Letter No. 32 from Alby to Henry
## (42 from Mull)

TELEPHONE:
STAGLAND 303

SOMEWHERE ON THE ISLE OF MULL
ARGYLL
SCOTLAND
5th December

Hello – Henry, are you there?

I could hear you roar last week. Rory said he heard something like a roar coming from your part of the world but he thought it might have been one of your ponies complaining about her dinner! Anyway, keep roaring every morning this week before you go to school. Someone is bound to hear you one of the days.

Henry, the funniest things have happened this week. All to do with the townies and Phil the Pheasant.

Phil is getting very old but he is very colourful and lives in the Torosay Gardens. The castle gardener, castle caretaker and their friends hunt him every Christmas but he always gets away.

Well – last Church-day, Roger the raven twig-radioed from Craignure that a party of townies had arrived on the ferry with a big van full of pheasants and pheasant food.

During the afternoon they carted their strange load up the Mossieburn almost as far our winter stag-house. Then they put all the food in little cans scattered about the wood, and let hundreds of men-as-well-as-lady-pheasants out of huge hampers. The pheasants didn't know where they were and hopped all over the wood looking for the tins of food. Then the townies packed up and went back to the hotel at Craignure.

We all watched with much amusement. Soon after the townies had gone, Phil flew in. We don't

130

*. . . Downstairs there was shambles . . .*

know him very well but sometimes he helps with Twig Radio. He wanted to know what all the farmyard-pheasants were doing in his woods.

The farmyard-pheasants didn't understand Phil's Mulloch accent and just went on guzzling the pheasant food. So Phil suddenly started chasing them with his ears sticking out and his hackles up. He screeched and roared as he pecked at the invaders.

After a little while, the invaders disappeared into the bracken in fear. Phil got going on the pheasant food, and the nobbers who were with us gave him a hand until there was none left.

Down in the hotel, the townies had got all dressed up for their dinner and were about to come down the stairs when there was crash on one of their windows. It was a pheasant which was trying to fly towards the bedroom light but hadn't seen the glass. The townies were amazed because they were at least two miles from the Mossieburn where they had let the pheasants loose – so they went downstairs to tell the others.

Downstairs there was shambles. There were pheasants everywhere – some sitting on the dining room tables – a few pushing the circular front door round and round so that more could come in. One was sitting on the manager's head. One was sitting on a spring bell hung on the wall which rang every time the pheasant moved – and there was a cock pheasant on the cash till which marked up another £1.50 each time he crowed!

Roger said it was the funniest sight he had ever seen.  .

Well, Henry, the manager and the chef and the barman all arrived with fish landing nets and tried to catch the pheasants but they wouldn't be caught. Instead they chased them into the circular door which they helped to keep moving so that the invaders were pushed out.

But every time they went out, they came back again, led on by the lights inside the hotel.

The manager had a great idea, Henry. He first told the townies to sit down. Then he turned off all the lights in the hotel and went to the car park where he turned on the headlights of his car. The light outside persuaded the pheasants to go outside.

When they got outside, they rushed to join many of their friends on the hotel roof or the roofs of cars in the car park. They all looked petrified, Henry, and it didn't take long to see why.

Sitting in the centre of the fence round the car park was Phil in all his glory. On either side of him, stretched along the top of the fence, were twenty other island cock pheasants. They all looked very fierce, Henry, and they were making a sort of chuck-chuck sound, and this frightened the invaders.

When the last pheasant had gone out, the manager turned off his headlights, shut all the hotel doors and turned on the lights again in the hotel.

After a while, the headwaiter came into the lounge and announced – 'Dinner is served'.

Whereupon there was a terrible noise of battle outside – feathers flew down the chimneys, pheazzies hit the windows and birds of all sorts screeched as you have never heard, Henry.

Phil had heard the announcement that 'dinner was served' and though it was meant for him to start his dinner – so he and his army had launched a vicious attack on the invaders.

The noise was so terrible that the townies could not hear themselves eat – so they waited for it to finish. Then they went outside with torches and picked up 122 invaders out of the 500 that had been brought over. There was no sign of Phil and his gang but the townies had pheazzie for dinner – with gravy and bread sauce.

That is not all that happened, Henry, but I must give this to the eagle-postman before he finds any pheazzies to eat. I'll tell you the rest in my next, Henry.

Be a good boy now,

Your old chum,

Alby

# Letter No. 33 from Alby to Henry

## (43 from Mull)

TELEPHONE:
STAGLAND 303

SOMEWHERE ON THE ISLE OF MULL
ARGYLL
SCOTLAND
12th December

Hello Henry,

Oh, those pheazzies – they are the stupidest birds. You remember I told you in my last letter about the carry-on at the hotel the night the pheazzies arrived. Well, listen to what happened the morning after.

We all had a good night's sleep, up in our Mossieburn home, but, in the morning, many of us had rather nasty headaches – and do you know why, Henry – because many of us woke up to find, one, two or even three pheazzies roosting on our horns.

I had a cock pheazzie on the top of my big right horn and a hen on the brow of my left horn – they were very heavy and wouldn't get off. Rory had one sitting on his head between his horns and Niall had one on each horn, one on his head and one on his back. All the pheazzies were asleep when we woke up.

Rory suggested we all jog-trotted round in a circle to see if the pheazzies would wake up and go away. This we did but, although all the pheazzies woke up, they wouldn't flyaway. Rory made us lift our knees higher and higher as we jogged but still the pheazzies hung on as though they were enjoying themselves. Suddenly Rory shouted 'JUMP' so we all jumped, and the pheazzies either fell off or flew off. Where they went to we didn't know except they headed down the Mossieburn – some flying, some on foot, and we were all left alone in peace to have our mossie-breakfast.

Just as we were finishing and settling down to chew the breakfast cud (you remember what chewing the cud means, Henry?) Roger the Raven flew in and said that Twig Radio reported eight Townies, each accompanied by a rough looking man carrying two guns, two cartridge bags, two mackintoshes and a game bag, getting out of the Land Rover on the road at the bottom of the Mossieburn. He also said that Eaglet Post had seen about twenty men walking up to the top of the Mossieburn wood with dogs and sticks. We knew they must be 'beaters', Henry, who were going to walk in a line through the Mossieburn woods and chase the poor farmyard pheazzies over the townies below, who would shoot at them as they flew over.

Niall thought the whole thing terrible and held a quick meeting of the smell-sentries to decide on how we could help the poor pheazzies.

We were all scratching our horns and thinking about what was the best thing to do when Phil glided in over the birch woods with two of his cock pheazzie friends. 'Leave it to me,' said Phil – and we said we would.

Then Phil and his two friends ran about in the bracken and managed to talk to many of the farmyard pheazzies. They explained to them that they were going to be chased by horrible hunters so that they flew over the townies who would shoot them. Phil told them that he was sorry about the night before – but now he and his chums were on their side and would help them escape from the townies. All they had to do was to take off when the 'beaters' arrived, then fly round in circles above the birch trees until they were all in the air, then follow Phil and his friends who would guide them to safety.

And so, Henry, we all waited to see what happened.

The 'beaters' arrived at the top of Mossieburn very close to us and lined out in a long line with their yapping dogs and faced downhill through the birch trees. Then a horn was heard from far away. Then one of the beaters blew another horn to let the townies know he had heard theirs.

*… The beaters arrived at the top of the Mossieburn …*

Then the 'beaters' started walking through the trees, hitting bracken with their sticks and encouraging their spaniels to hunt out the wretched farmyard pheazzies.

As the spaniels found a pheazzie, it took to the wing and flew round and round above the birch trees.

Henry, by the time the 'beaters' had got to the bottom of the hill, the townies had not fired a single shot, and there were 378 pheazzies flying round and round above the birch trees.

It was then that Phil and his two chums appeared. They flew very slowly through the pheazzies that were going round and round. One after another the farmyard pheazzies followed on until there was a huge flock of 378 farmyard pheazzies following Phil and his chums – not over the townies but back over Ben More. It was a long pull up for the invaders but they made it, and when they were over the top, they floated down directly towards Craignure.

Phil led them on and on – out over the sea towards Oban. Then he and his two friends suddenly left them, wishing them good-luck and telling them to fly on to Oban and make a new home on the mainland.

But as the pheazzies flew on, so they got tireder and tireder. One or two of them collapsed and landed in the sea – but most of them managed to glide on until the Oban ferry was below them – then they all swooped down on the boat and perched on the masts, the rigging, the funnels – anywhere. And the boat steamed on for Oban.

Well, Henry, that is all we know. Phil is back in Torosay and the ferry carried the farmyard pheazzies to the mainland – what happened to them then, I have no idea.

All we do know is that the townies went back to the mainland on the next ferry. They had spent a lot of their money in order to shoot these poor farmyard pheazzies but they hadn't shot one.

Some of the townies had to spend the night in Oban and went to a restaurant for dinner – where they were given roast pheazzie with bread sauce – for the second night running. I wonder where the restaurant owner got the pheazzies, don't you, Henry?

And so Phil saved some of the farmyard pheazzies but also made certain that none of them stayed on the Island – it would have been terrible if they had – they couldn't even speak Mullach – could they, Henry?

It's snowing now. I suppose because it's getting close to Christmas.

I hope you have got a hole in your stocking, Henry, otherwise Father Christmas won't be able to fill it, will he?

Night, night – your old grunt-grunt,

Alby

135

# Letter No. 34 from Alby to Henry

## (No 44 from Mull)

TELEPHONE:
STAGLAND 303

SOMEWHERE ON THE ISLE OF MULL
ARGYLL
SCOTLAND
19th December

Hello Henry.

It's very cold here, and we are still too weak to do much jogging. However, we do a quick trot round the Professor's teaching-moss each morning, and that helps to keep us warm. Rory is in charge of the new nobbers, and he has them jogging for an hour each day. He makes them grunt the Jogging Song while they jog!

Next week it is Stag-Christmas, and everyone in Stagland and everyone in your land will be going to Church-day-Service and thanking deer-God for the good news of love and fellowship which His Son, Jesus Christ, spread amongst peoples.

The young nobbers will be hanging up their cast-off velvet stockings on the birch trees, hoping that Father Christmas and his reindeer will come by and pop some little prezzy into them as a special goodwill gift.

Yesterday at stag-school, just before breaking up for Father Christmas holidays, the Professor told the young nobber class all about Father Christmas.

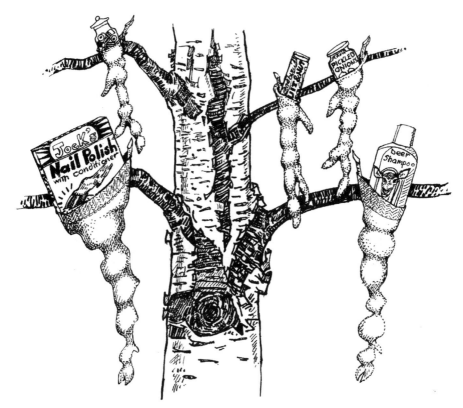

*... The young nobbers will be hanging up their cast-off velvet stockings ...*

This is what he said, Henry.

'It was a long, long time ago, way up in the-North of the world, in wintertime, when it was all dark and cold with snow and ice everywhere, that an old farmer, called Nicky, sat down by the whale-oil fire in his igloo (snow house) and wondered how he could help young nobbers to be grateful for all Stag-Jesus had done for us,

'He decided that the best way would be to see that all nobbers got presents on the day of Stag-Jesus' birth. This would give them something to be grateful for, and, at the same time, remember Stag-Jesus. But he knew that he could not manage to organise this from his igloo on the North end of the world so he called in his six favourite reindeer-stags and asked them what they thought.

'The reindeer all thought that the farmer had a splendid idea but it was going to be a big problem to make presents for all nobbers in the world during the eleven months before Stag-Christmas, and then to have them delivered all over the world on Stag-Christmas Eve, considering they had only one sledge, six reindeer and their farmer master to do it.

'Eventually the biggest reindeer suggested they write down on non-melting ice everything that would have to be done to carry out the plan. He would then tie the bit of ice to his back with thick, thick wire so that when the time came for him to climb up to be with Stag-Jesus and the Flying Jumbos, he would be sure to take it with him.

137

*... Henry at home on Christmas morning ...*

'The Reindeer knew that, through time, his master and his Reindeer friends would join him in Skyland where the Flying Jumbos fly, and where there should be masses of room to work, hundreds and hundreds of Stag-people to make presents and endless reindeer to deliver them on Stag-Christmas Eve.

'All was agreed by the old farmer as he warmed his hands by the fire, so they wrote out their plan on a bit of non-melting ice and tied it on the back of the biggest reindeer.

'It took almost ten years before the farmer and all six Reindeer had got to Stag-Jesus land where the Flying Jumbos fly.

'When they did get there, they studied the plan on the bit of non-melting ice and set up huge workshops in Jumbo-land, to make toys during the eleven months before Stag-Christmas so they could be ready for delivery on Stag-Christmas Eve. Then they organised teams of reindeer and farmer drivers to drive the presents all over the world, in their sleighs sucked along by the Jumbo vapour trails.    :

'As they got to stag-forests, they dropped their prezzies down the side of the birch tree-trunks so that they fell in the nobbers' velvet stockings.

'And they did the same thing for the two-legged human nobbers, except that, in their case, the farmer drivers climbed down the townie chimneys and put the prezzies in the nobbers' stockings which they had hung on their beds. Sometimes they found a note asking for something special, in which case the farmer had to climb all the way up the chimney again to get the special present.

'Now you know one of the reasons why all nobbers want to say "Thank-you" to dear-deer-God for sending His Son, Stag-Jesus-Christ, to help us. If we had never heard of Him, there would have been no Christmas and, therefore, no prezzies.

'The farmer had one more wish. He wanted any plant used for Christmas decoration to be spring-like – not winter-like – so that we could look forward to the lovely months ahead.

'Therefore, all plants and trees used for Christmas decorations were to be green the fir tree, the holly, the mistletoe and even the water-lily.

'As Nicky, the old farmer had been so kind to all God's children, he was made a Saint and was known as Saint Nicholas. He grew a white beard and always wore a red cloak and hood with white fur trimmings. He is now known as Father Christmas all over the world.'

Professor Red Deer finished his talk by wishing the whole school a very Happy Stag-Christmas and told the nobbers not to forget to buy their Mummies and Daddies a little something to celebrate the birth of Stag-Jesus with.

Next week Henry, I'll tell you what happened on Stag-Christmas Day in the stag herd on Ben More.

Meanwhile, I hope you remember to leave a note by the fireplace, addressed to Father Christmas and telling him what he should leave in your stocking. You might like to leave a wee glass of GLENLIVET as well to warm the cockles of the old man's heart.

Don't forget to hang up your stocking, Henry, and don't forget why the old farmer organised all this – it was to be sure that the young people all over the world are grateful for Stag-Jesus-Christ, or, as you call Him, Little-Lord-Jesus.

Here comes Golden Eagle Post. His bag full of letters and parcels with holly leaves all round them.

Happy Christmas, Henry.

Your old friend,

Alby

*… Christmas day in the forest …*

# Letter No. 35 from Alby to Henry

## (No 45 from Mull)

TELEPHONE:
STAGLAND 303

SOMEWHERE ON THE ISLE OF MULL
ARGYLL
SCOTLAND
26th December

Noel, Noel Henry,

That means Happy Christmas, Happy Christmas and I hope you had a really happy happy day with plenty of prezzies from Father Christmas and Mum and Dad and others. The weather was booful here; snow all round, blue skies and frost.

We had a very special Church-day Service in the Mossieburn, Henry and the whole of Ben More Stagland was there.

The new nobbers performed a Nativity Play. That is acting out the story of the Stag-Shepherds and the Wise Stags and Stag-Joseph and Hind-Mary and the first days of the little Stag-Jesus.

First of all three nobbers, pretending to be stag-shepherds, lay down amongst some of Hamish's sheep. Then Rory and Niall grunted very loudly, Ronnie the Roe whistled, and all the birds tweeted at the same time. This represented the arrival of the hind-angel of the Stag-Lord. From behind a large tree root a huge stag-policeman grunted out:

'Go to Bunessan where you will find a baby stag-calf resting in a myrtle bog with his hind-mummy by his side. This calf will grow into our Stag-Saviour – a great stag far greater even than THE MONARCH' – and then there was silence.

140

*... And produced lovely prezzies of green moss, blaeberries and rhubarb leaves ...*

The three shepherds got up, grunted a few grunts to each other and jogged towards us (pretending we were at Bunessan) and there, curled up in a bit of Bog Myrtle was the youngest stag-calf we could find, with his Mummy acting as Mary on one side and Rory, acting as Joseph, on the other. The shepherds were so excited that they bent their front legs and wagged their tails – grunting that they would go and tell everyone on the hill what they had seen – the Saviour of all Stagland. And after a little while they jog-trotted out over the hill.

As soon as they had gone, three very wise looking stags came out of the trees on our right (they had 'WISE' written on their rumps) and they went up to Niall who was acting the part of Herod, the King, who was very jealous of Stag-Jesus, Henry. They grunted to him that they had heard that the greatest stag ever had been born. They grunted that he would be a greater stag even than Herod, and this made Herod very angry. But the three wise stags didn't know exactly where this baby stag had been born so Herod went off to ask Professor Red Deer if he knew (he was acting the part of a High-Priest). The Professor grunted 'In Bunessan'. So Herod told the three wise-stags to go to Bunessan, find the baby stag and bring him back to Herod so that he could meet him – and probably kill him, Henry.

Olly the Owl, who was in a very high birch tree to the East of all the deer, turned on his eye-lights, which he normally used at night, and pointed them at the three wise stags: who started to walk towards the light. (It was supposed to be the star in the East, Henry, which had guided the Wise Stags all the way to Bunessay and was now going to guide them to the exact Myrtle bog where the baby stag was lying.) The wise stags followed Olly's lights which guided them to where the baby stag was lying.

Then the three wise stags bent their front knees and wagged their tails three times and produced lovely prezzies of green moss, blaeberries and rhubarb leaves they had pinched from Torosay gardens, and then – and then – and then, there was another terrible grunt and whistle and tweet, and the stag-policeman boomed out:

'Don't tell stag-Herod where you found the calf – he is a nasty – rather go back to your homes in the west' – and then silence once more.

The three wise stags walked backwards from the Myrtle bog and weren't seen again.

After a few moments an old, old stag, called Simon, appeared on four crutches and staggered up to the calf.

'You are the Son of dear-deer-God,' he grunted, 'dear-deer-God who promised I should see you before I went up to the Flying Jumbos,' and he licked the baby stag all over. Then he looked up to the blue sky just as a Jumbo flew by leaving lovely vapour trials.

'Now I have seen you,' he grunted, 'I am ready to go to Jumbo-Land,' and with that he vanished. (He didn't really, Henry, he just fell down in a huge bush of rushes so that no one could see him.)

We all clapped our front feet together as a way of congratulating Niall and the nobbers on their fine performance.

After a pause, Professor Red Deer stood on his rock and told us we had just seen the story of the beginning of Stag-Jesus. He reminded us that he had told us how Stag Jesus ended the first part of his life in Stagland at the Stag-Easter Service on April 8th.

(You remember in my letter that week I told you all about the Stag-Easter Service and what the Professor told us, Henry – how Stag-Jesus was killed by the horrible switches and then came back to teach us more about dear-deer-God, finally climbing up and up to where the Jumbos fly.)

All this happened at our Church-day Service, Henry, and when the play was over, we grunted the most beautiful hymn.

> Away in a peat bog, no moss for a bed,
> The little Stag-Jesus laid down his sweet head
> The stars in the bright sky shone down on his feet.
> The little Stag-Jesus asleep on the peat.
>
> The sheep are ba-baa-ing, the calfie awakes,
> The little Stag-Jesus no grunting He makes,
> We love Thee Stag-Jesus. Look down from the sky
> And stay by our sides until morning is nigh.

Be near us Stag-Jesus, we ask Thee to stay
Close by us forever and love us we pray.
Bless all our dear Calfies in Thy tender care
And fit them for blue skies to live with Thee there.

And at the end we grunted a big AMEN.

So ended Stag-Christmas morning, Henry. We all went back to our mossie places and had huge lunches. In the afternoon, most of us went to sleep or chewed the cud, but Rory took some of the new nobbers off to teach them how to play leap-frog and blind-stag's buff. I was worried for a bit in case he took them to Torosay, but he didn't. You see, Henry, Rory is getting very wise now and he is very proud of being head Prefect at school.

Now I'm off to a Christmas Grunting Concert in Mossieburn. Next week I'll tell you how we get on on New Year's Eve,

More Noels and big grunts,

*Alby*

P. S. The only bit of sad news is that I hear The Monarch still hasn't been found. Rory says he saw Trash the other day and asked him, but all Trash did was to walk away with his tail between his legs again. He must know something, Henry. Surely The Monarch hasn't been sausaged.

P. p. S. Here comes old Golden Eagle Post. He looks as though he's had far too many plum-myxie-rabbits, but he'll get to you in time.

# Letter No. 3 from Rory to Henry

## (46 from Mull)

TELEPHONE:
STAGLAND 303

SOMEWHERE ON THE ISLE OF MULL
ARGYLL
SCOTLAND
2nd January

Hi-de-hi, Henry

Grandpa Alby said he was going to tell you all about our Stag New Year's Eve but he had to go away in a hurry and left me to tell you the story.

But, first of all, Grandpa Alby had to go away because the Lord-Stag-Chamber-Lain came over on Stag New Year's Eve to say that there was still no sign of The Monarch. He said he was organising a search by all herds on the Island, and please would Grandpa Alby and some stags from Ben More help, so that is where he has gone. Niall and nine others have gone with him. I expect he will write you himself next week, Henry, and tell you how the search went – but all stag-persons on the Island are very, very worried in case The Monarch has been sausaged.

Well, now, New Year's Eve. All the stag herd on Ben More started with a huge meal of rhubarb leaves, water lilies, oats, turnips and special green moss which had either been collected from the gardens round Craignure by the new nobbers or given to them by folk who wanted to send messages of goodwill to the stag herd.

Then we all split up to go first-footing, Henry – that is to be the first people to cross the front moss-step of friends around the Island.

I went down with two bags of wood as goodwill presents to the naughty nobbers of Bunessan. Only one was there – the other had gone off to help find The Monarch. We had a wonderful evening, Henry – dancing the horn dance and grunting Mulloch Airs and playing hide-and-seek. We ate masses of good food, and I didn't get back to Ben More until just before sunrise. I had hoped to meet the booful two-year-old, but she had gone off with a new big boyfriend from Cairn Ban.

Another party of young stags went off to Cairn Ban where they saw the booful hind jog-trotting with her new nobber friend. Then they saw the two of them go to the Fairies Circle and kneel down on their forelegs and wish – I wonder what for – don't you, Henry? I was very jealous when I heard about this and can't wait to hear who this new nobber friend was.

Yet another party went off to Laggan Forest to wish the stag herd there a Happy New
Year, but it was all quiet and sad, Henry, as The Monarch was missing.

When everyone had finished their visits, they came back to Ben More to rejoin our stag herd. Many stags from other herds who had been visiting us on Ben More spent all night here.

After we all got back, the party really got going. We had the grunting choir grunting old Stagland songs. We had Professor Red Deer telling us stories of the past. We had little plays acted by the new nobbers, and then we all sang songs together until the sun rose above Oban. At the end of it all, Henry, we stood on our back legs, crossed our front legs and sang:

> Should auld a-roaring be forgot
> And never roared again,
> Should. auld a-roaring be forgot,
> In spite of all the rain
> We'll take a drop of Mossburn Moss
> And drink it down with plea ... jar,
> In this year we'll ne'er be cross,
> Yet friendship we'll just trea ... jar.

Then we all walked round and shook each other by the forefoot, wishing each other Happy New Year. We went on grunting to each other until well after daylight.

It was a great evening of friendship, Henry, extending across the Stag herds on the Island. We were all grateful for the Stagland we lived in and for the friendship we enjoyed.

Ronnie and Gorkie and Roger and Harold the Hare, and the Bunnies and Olly and even Freddie the Fox joined in our singing. Away in the distance we could hear the fiddles playing reels in Hamish's cottage where there was dancing and singing all the night through. We could also hear poor old Trash wailing a lament and begging the shepherds to go to bed soon!

It must have been about three hours after sunrise, when we were all fast asleep, that we were wakened by footsteps in the snow.

I looked up, Henry, and there was Grandpa Alby.

'Any news?' I grunted.

*... Should auld a-roaring be forgot ...*

'None,' came the reply.

'Where is Niall, my Dad!' I asked.

'Still looking,' answered Grandpa Alby, and with that he slumped down on a bit of snow covered moss and went to sleep.

Henry, the only person who has not been taking part in the celebrations is Golden Eagle Post. He had had an upset tummy after too many myxie rabbits. However, he promised he will get this to you as it is New Year – even if he has to walk.

Happy New Year, Henry. Happy New Year, Henry's Dad. Happy New Year, Henry's Mum – Happy New Year from me and my Dad Niall, and my Granddad Alby, and all the stags and hinds and birds and fish on Ben More in Stagland on the Island of Mull.

Your playmate

# Rory

P. S. Golden Eagle Post says that. Mr MacTavish, Hamish and Trash also send messages of Goodwill for the New Year.

# Letter No. 36 from Alby to Henry

## (47 from Mull)

TELEPHONE:
STAGLAND 303

SOMEWHERE ON THE ISLE OF MULL
ARGYLL
SCOTLAND
9th January

Henry,

I, can hardly say Hello, I am so tired. We have been looking for The Monarch day after day but no sign. We all thought he must have been sausaged. Then last night we heard through Twig radio the sad story of how Trash had found him.

I believe the Professor told you the first part of the story some weeks ago of how Trash had found The Monarch wounded by another stag in a fight-and how he had promised to go back and see him again after Stag-New-Year.

Well, Henry – on Stag-New-Year's Eve, after Hamish had stopped playing his fiddle and gone to bed, Trash broke out of his kennel and trudged off through the snow to the Laggan Forest. When he got there, he lay down and rested until daybreak, then he searched the snowy peat hags in the area where he had last seen The Monarch but he was nowhere to be found. For three days he wandered about looking, and for three days he avoided being seen by the stag-search party. Then, on the fourth day, he was just about to go back home, tired and weary, when his paw hit something sharp in the snow.

Trash scraped round the something sharp which he had struck with his paw, and yes, it was, Henry – it was – it was the top cup of a huge stag's horn – and it wasn't very far from where, he had last seen The Monarch.

Trash scraped with his paws and dug with his paws and bit with his teeth. Slowly he made a hole deep enough to see the stag's head at the end of the horn. He dug and scraped at the snow and ice with all four legs for almost a day. By nightfall he was sure he had found all that was left of The Monarch – the rest had gone to join the flying Jumbos.

Trash didn't know what to do, Henry. He decided to try and gnaw the top off one of the horns and take it back to be identified by someone who had known The Monarch well. So he gnawed and gnawed and gnawed for six hours and at last a top broke off in his mouth – but by this time Trash was very hungry and very, very tired – and it was dark. Very slowly he stumbled through the snow carrying the bit of horn but, just before daylight, he collapsed. He was so tired he couldn't go any further.

Meanwhile Hamish and Mr MacTavish were in a terrible state, not knowing where Trash had gone to. Everyone was looking for everyone. The stags were looking for their Monarch, the shepherds were looking for Trash, and Trash was looking for someone to tell where The Monarch was.

When dawn came, Golden Eagle Post happened to be looking for a mousie or two for his eaglets when he spotted Trash asleep in the snow. He swooped down and pecked him. Trash woke up and told Golden Eagle Post the story. He had proof in his mouth that he had found The Monarch but it seemed such a long time ago, he couldn't remember where he had found him.

*… He spotted Trash alsleep in the snow …*

Golden Eagle Post said he would take the top of The Monarch's horn to the Lord-Stag-Chamber-Lain for identification, and this would let Trash go home to his master. They both went on their ways.

When trash got home, Hamish gave him a big bone for his din-dins and wrapped him up with fresh straw in his kennel so that he could have a good rest.

As soon as the Lord-Stag-Chamber-Lain saw the bit of horn, he identified it as belonging to the dead Monarch and went to tell Professor Red Deer at the Mossieburn. He suggested that they sat down and worked out who was to be the new Monarch according to the law of the forest. But the Professor said he had already worked that out because he had been almost certain that The Monarch was dead for some time although he had no proof.

The next day was a sad, sad day when all stags were informed about what had happened. The whole of Stagland went into mourning, and the smell sentries wore black horn bands.

Professor Red Deer sent a message out by Twig Radio, asking all stags to look up as the next flying Jumbo passed overhead leaving its vapour trails in the blue, blue sky, and to remember with gratitude all that great stag from Laggan had done for the forest over the many years he had been Monarch. And this we all did.

I am your rather weary chum,

# Alby

P. S. Trash told me, when I met him on the hill the day after The Monarch's death had been announced, that The Monarch must have died from wounds suffered after fighting a big, big, stag. He couldn't have been the big stag I fought, could he, Henry? The one I went to tell The Monarch about – remember, Henry? – but The Monarch wasn't there to apologise to – remember, Henry? Henry, did I, Alby, kill The Monarch?

*… Did I, Alby, kill the Monarch …*

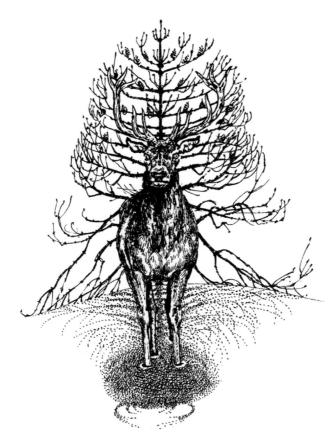

# Letter No. 37 from Alby to Henry

## (48 from Mull)

TELEPHONE:
STAGLAND 303

SOMEWHERE ON THE ISLE OF MULL
ARGYLL
SCOTLAND
16th January

Henry,

I am a very worried stag. Do you think I killed The Monarch? If so, what should I do; to fight one of one's best friends is bad enough but to fight him to the death is terrible, even if it did happen at a time when nature says we must go half mad.

Oh, one moment, Henry – something very odd is happening as I write this. I see a great procession of stags coming up Ben More from the South – some seem to be dancing and grunting the Jogging Song. They all look very happy. It must be somebody's birthday or something.

Anyway, it's a beautiful frosty day, and I can relax, chew the cud and try to remember more about that fight with the big stag in October.

Sorry about this muddled up letter, Henry, but I'm still worried about this procession. I see the Lord-Stag-Chamber-Lain is in front with – with – with – yes it is, Henry, he's with Professor Red Deer – what are they playing at? I see one or two hinds with them as well. They are singing and dancing like mad. Oh, Henry, they are heading straight for me. I will have to stop writing now and finish this letter after I have found out what it is all about.

Henry, this is two hours later – two very difficult hours they were too. I'm sure you will have many difficult situations to face, and you will face them very well, but I find difficult situations very, very difficult to face. This is what happened.

As soon as I put my heather pen and paper away, all the smell sentries stood up and the Professor, with the Lord-Stag-Chamber-Lain, came up to me and bowed very low indeed, wagging their tails. I didn't know what to do so I bowed back.

Then Professor Red Deer opened a huge scroll of bracken paper and grunted with Deep Grunts:

'I, the senior Professor in the Stagland of Mull, together with my colleague the Lord Stag-Chamber-Lain, do hereby announce that, after careful research, we are satisfied that you Royal Alby are henceforth really royal. You have not only beaten the old Monarch in battle, but you also came from a good family and have a Monarch's head. In other words, Sire, we have to announce to all Stags and Hinds and Birds and Bunnies and Sheep and Shepherds and Woofers and Lairds and horrible Hunters and horrible hunters' horses that you, this day, have been proclaimed MONARCH OF THE FOREST, and we hereby invite you formally to accept the appointment, knowing that you will have the total support of all Stagland, and that your Court will be moved from Laggan to Ben More forthwith.'

There was a pause and then he grunted

'Sire, will you accept?'

Well, Henry, what was I to do. Here was I, possibly killer of the last Monarch, one of my best friends, being asked to be the next Monarch.

I stood up with all the dignity I could muster and looked the Professor and then the Lord-Stag-Chamber-Lain in the eyes. Then I looked all round the booful stags who were all looking at me and waiting for me to agree – then I grunted with a big grunt.

'Wait – I must consider what you have asked me. Please come back at the same time today-week when I will give you an answer.'

The crowd never expected me to say that, Henry. They expected me to agree, and they were already to clap and cheer and fix the date for the Monarch-ation. (Like your Coronation, Henry). The Professor and the Chamber-Lain didn't expect it either and looked very puzzled. Then the crowd all turned down the hill and went back to their herds, while the Professor and the Chamber-Lain asked me to come into the birch woods with them.

When we were out of sight, the Professor turned on me.

'Why did you do that, Alby?' he grunted, 'we have looked through all the tree-bark files and you are undoubtedly the rightful Monarch from every point of view. Anyway you would be a wonderful one. You are a great fighter and a great leader and those lovely horns are going to get more magnificent every year.'

I looked the Professor up and down.

'Would you want a stag who had skewered his best friend to death as your Monarch?'

I grunted.

'Alby,' grunted the Professor, 'the law of the forest dictates that, at certain times of the year, we stags go mad and we fight to the death, if necessary, to satisfy our desires. We don't think about

*… The Lord Chamberlain and the Professor trotting off …*

friends or compassion or pain. We just fight. It seems that you fought the Monarch for his hinds with great skill and bravery – two qualities the old Monarch admired most. I'll tell you something else,' said the Professor, 'you may have beaten the old Monarch in battle but you did not kill him.'

'How do you know I didn't kill him,' I grunted. 'Trash thinks I did.'

'We will give you proof that you didn't next week,' grunted the Professor.

'I will need proof in public,' I grunted. 'All those lovely stag-people who came up in the procession will have to be given the proof as well when they come back next week.'

'Very well,' grunted the Professor. 'This will be done.' And he and the Chamber- Lain trotted off.

I was so worried, I quickly went off and saw Niall and Rory and Olly in case they knew why the Professor was so certain that I hadn't killed the Monarch, but they didn't. What is more, Olly twigged round all the members of twig radio and no one knew.

I don't think I will sleep tonight, Henry. I'll keep this letter until morning.


Now it's morning. I didn't go to sleep. I just walked round and round the birchwood wondering.

Niall had said he didn't think it mattered even if I had killed The Monarch because it was done at a time of madness. But this didn't appeal to me – one should never do anything nasty, not even in a time of madness, Henry.

Everything was going round and round in my head, and my antlers were hurting.

Ronnie the Roe came by to say how much the Roe deer in the Island hoped I would become Monarch – nice chap, Ronnie – and then he said he would give this to Golden Eagle Post when he went by the Myxie Garage. So I gave it to him while I go on wondering.

Next week I should know more, Henry.

Your very unsettled chum

Alby

*… Jeannie remembers the Monarch …*

# Letter No. 38 from Alby to Henry

## (49 from Mull)

TELEPHONE:
STAGLAND 303

SOMEWHERE ON THE ISLE OF MULL
ARGYLL
SCOTLAND
23rd January

Hello Henry,

This has been a terrible week of worrying and wondering but now all is settled and this is how it happened.

Two days after Church-day, I was told that representatives of the herds in Stagland would come to the top of Ben More as the sun was at its highest – same as they did last week – and the Professor would prove that I did not kill The Monarch.

All went according to plan, but more stag-people came than last week, Henry.

When all were assembled, the Professor stood on a large stone behind me and called for silence. Then out of the birch trees came the smallest hind calf you have ever seen. She was thin and weak and wobbly but she managed to get to the Professor who put his foreleg over her neck to comfort her. Then he started:

'Alby and friends, this is Jeannie. She comes from the Laggan herd and was born of a famous Laggan hind.

'Soon after Trash had seen The Monarch all wounded and sore, Jeannie's Mum was sausaged by the horrible hunters, but they didn't sausage her. They left her to make her own way in the forest. The hind herd galloped off when the shot rang out, leaving her all alone watching her Mum being carried away. She was only four months old at the time and very, very sad. There was little strength in her, so she just lay down on her own in the snow, crying – and then she went to sleep.

'When dawn came she was woken by footsteps, and standing beside her was the biggest stag she had ever seen. Now she says she is strong enough to tell all that followed.'

The Professor led the baby hind up on to the stone and grunted "Speak up little lady", and the little lady spoke up.

'The big stag asked me who I was and where I came from. I told him all. He said he had been hurt in a fight with another big stag some weeks before and he thought he was going to join the flying Jumbos but was so very much better now and was making his way back to his herd in Laggan. He said the stag he had been fighting was one of the most booful in the Forest.

'He said he would take me with him and see that I was looked after – so we set off – very slowly. I was weak, and he was still a bit stiff in the joints. It was snowing.

*... It all happened so suddenly ...*

'After we had been going about half an hour alongside the Pennyghael Road, a car drew up and a horrible hunter pushed a rifle out of the window. BANG.

'It all happened so suddenly, and I didn't realise what the bang was for a moment or two but a bullet had gone straight through the big stag's tum-tum. He started to trot, then to walk, then to walk more slowly, then he stopped and stood, then he walked, then he stood again, then he walked again. More bullets came after him but they all missed, and soon we were over a ridge.

'The big stag looked at me and said he knew he was on his way to the Flying Jumbos this time but he must go back to where Trash had found him so that he would find him again.

'I didn't know who Trash was then, and the big stag was getting very croaky. However, he turned back in what was now a snowstorm and walked slowly on for about an hour. Then he grunted "This will do", and lay down in a big peat hag.

'He told me he hadn't got much longer in the Forest and asked me to stay with him until he left for the Jumbos. He told me to fight my way against the wind after he had left and to climb the biggest hill that lay ahead. He told me to go on climbing until I got to the top, and there I would find a very friendly stag herd who would help. He told me to ask for the Professor.

'I stayed with him for something like another hour, and the snowstorm cleared and the sun came out. Pointing to a big hill to the North, the old stag said – "There is Ben More, that is the hill you must climb – go now while the sun is out". I begged to be allowed to stay with him to the end, as he had originally asked, but he said "No" – so I started to walk away. As I did so I heard a big grunt and looked back to see the old stag on his side – he had joined the Jumbos. I went back to him and licked his nose and left for the top of Ben More. I didn't get here for nearly two days and, when I did, I was put in the Mossiospital to recover, where I told my story to Professor Red Deer.'

'Thank you,' grunted the Professor. 'Now you see, Alby, the old Monarch was shot – you did not kill him.'

'What is your decision? Do you accept that you are our Monarch?'

I waited a moment, Henry. The story we had just heard was so very sad but I knew then that I must say 'Yes'. It was my duty to the herd and to Stagland in Mull.

I beckoned Jeannie, the baby hind, over – and held her with my foreleg and then, squeezing her, gave a great big grunt 'I AGREE'.

You have never heard such a noise as followed, Henry. Every animal, bird and bee in Mull cheered with great big grunts. Then every stag-person in sight bowed and wagged their tails. Then the Lord-Stag-Chamber-Lain grunted to the crowd that the date of the Monarch-ation would be announced shortly and the crowd went back to their herd houses.

Soon I realised I was alone at the top of Ben More with Jeannie. There were six smell sentries surrounding me. I was a very important stag-person with a very important job to do.

Next week I'll tell you about the arrangements for the Monarch-ation.

Your old friend,

Alby

*… Alone at the top of Ben More with Jeannie and six smell sentries …*

*... The new Lord Chamberlain and Stag-Querry ...*

# Letter No. 39 from Alby to Henry

## (50 from Mull)

TELEPHONE:
STAGLAND 303

SOMEWHERE ON THE ISLE OF MULL
ARGYLL
SCOTLAND
30th January

Hello Henry,

I feel kind of moussy-moussy and awkward and wondering if I have done the right thing by agreeing to be Monarch.

It is a terrible responsibility and a terrible decision to have made, but in this life, Henry, we have to make terrible decisions and take on terrible responsibilities, and we do feel moussy-moussy and awkward for a little while. It's better than avoiding everything and accepting nothing – taking the sort of easy way out – then one turns into a bit of useless brown moss. From now on, I just have to do my 'best' for Stagland – I can no better.

Anyway, this week we have been making plans for the Monarch-ation which takes place next week, here on Ben More. I was worried in case it had to be at Laggan in the deep Corrie, but the Professor says it's quite all right to have it here.

Last Church-day I saw the last Monarch's Lord-Stag-Chamber-Lain and all the people that had looked after him so well. I thanked them and told them to go back and help in their own herd

157

at Laggan as I would be appointing my own helpers out of the Ben More herd. It was all rather sad as they were a very nice lot of stag-people but that is the way things go.

Then I started appointing my own helpers. I asked Niall to be my Chamberlain. He was thrilled and bowed to the ground. Then I asked Rory to be my head stag-querry he has to see that I get round the other herds on time and that I have the right stag-badges on, and he has to look very smart at all times. I think he'll do it very well. I asked dear old Morag to organise The Monarch's First Aid Corps. They will patch me up if I slip on a wet stone or do something stupid like that. The only other appointment I made was a special one for Jeannie – 'The Monarch's Little Maid'. It will make her feel important, and she will come to all big stag-occasions.

Niall and Rory are preparing the detailed plans for next Church-day – the Monarchation. It is to be when the sun is at it's highest. All Stagland is to come. Twig Radio are to let Mr MacTavish and Trash and Fergie and the head-keeper-hunter know that they are invited. Professor Red Deer will carry out the ceremony, and the head musical grunter will teach the twee-grunting choir how to sing 'Staggalleuya, Staggalleuya'.

A large number of nobbers have been told to go out all over the Island and collect masses of rhubarb leaves, water lilies and grain and all things succulent for the staganquet which is to follow the Service.

Rory and some of his friends are going to give a short display of stag dancing before the Stagbanquet.

The head policeman, whose name escapes me, is arranging for smell-sentries to come up to the Ben early in the morning to take up their positions all around our little corrie at the top of the Mossieburn so that the stag-herds won't have to bother about guards when they arrive.

I am going to make a special speech to the whole of Stagland on the day after Church-day, which will be broadcast on Twig Radio.

Henry, there is a great air of excitement everywhere.

We did have one little problem yesterday. Two silly two-legged nobber-boys came out from Craignure to slide on the ice on Loch Visa. Well, the ice wasn't thick enough far out, and one of them, who was trying to show off to the other, slid a long way out, broke the ice, fell in and, Henry, he might easily have been drowned. His chum went to his help and tried to pull him out

*… Were hanging on to each other's tails …*

but he fell in as well. They both screamed at the top of their voices, and one of our smell-sentries heard the cries so Rory and six young stags galloped down to help them. Poor lads, they were terrified. They couldn't get out because their hands kept on slipping on the ice.

Rory, who had been on a Red-Deer-Upside-Down Course and knew a bit about rescue work, told the young stags to line up one behind the other and catch on to the each other's tails (rather like Tolly-Trout's brother's friends did – do you remember, Henry?).

Then Rory walked onto the ice. It broke and each time he got back on to it, it broke again until he slowly made a sort of channel all the way out to the screaming lads. By the time he got there, all six young stags behind him were hanging on to each other's tail and up to their waists in water. Rory, being furthest out, was up to his neck.

Rory leant forward with his six smart points, and each boy, in turn, caught hold of a horn and pulled himself on to Rory's back. All they had to do then was to walk along the back of the six stags and jump onto the shore. They were blue with cold but very grateful to the staggies. Rory came ashore and gave them a terrible grunt never to be so stupid again, and after seeing the boys safely to the road and on to their bicycles, led the staggies back up the Ben. He had successfully carried out the first rescue of my reign, and I was proud of him.

So, Henry, think of me next Church-day. I wish you could be here with your Dad and Mum and Grandpas and Grannies and Fred and Olly. I will think of you – it will be a great day – I am very excited!

Yours,

Alby

*... Jeannie and the snow stag! ...*

*... Professor, New Monarch and New Chamberlain ...*

# Letter No. 40 from Alby to Henry

## (51 from Mull)

TELEPHONE:
STAGLAND 303

SOMEWHERE ON THE ISLE OF MULL
ARGYLL
SCOTLAND
6th February

Henry,

Last day-before-Church-day I dreamt about my Monarch-ation which was due to take place next day. The dream went like this:

There was snow on the ground, blue skies, frost and several flying jumbos flying overhead with big long vapour trails left behind them. It was a really booful day.

The church bells on the Island were ringing, and I was so lick-polished that stag-people could see their faces in me. I was sitting on the big stone at the head of the corrie above the Mossieburn with Rory, my stag-querry and wee Jeannie. Many, many stag-peoples from all over the island had come to our corrie and were lying all round the tops. Every birch tree had members of twig-radio perching on it, and there were more gliding about overhead. All the small animals were sitting round the rocks behind me, and old Gorkie the Grouse with Miss Partridge were on a rock just to my left.

I could hear the big stag-choir singing 'Staggalleuya, Staggalleuya' as they came closer, walking slowly up the burn, and I could see Niall, my new Lord-Stag-Chamber-Lain walking backwards at the head of the procession. It was a really lovely sight, Henry, and in my dreams I prayed to dear-deer-God with all my heart, thanking Him for all those wonderful friends on this wonderful Island with its wonderful hills and wonderful birch trees. And I begged him to let me do a really good job for Stagland, helping all the people there to lead happy and useful lives. I felt so very full of gratitude, Henry.

As the procession of the choir and representatives from all Stag Councils got closer, the music got louder. I think Jeannie was rather frightened because she started to nuzzle her nose into my side. I was rather frightened too, Henry – it was such an important occasion.

At last the Lord-Stag-Chamber-Lain's back legs were only feet away from me. He stopped, turned round, bowed low and wagged his tail. Then the whole crowd – everyone, Henry – did the same thing and gave a huge grunt, grunt, grunt as they did it. It was a terrific noise. I got up, looked all round, paused, and then did the same as they had done.

Professor Red Deer came out from the birch trees behind with a small procession, and I turned round to meet him. I lowered my head as he grunted very loudly

'In accordance with the wishes of all Stagland, you, great Alby, are appointed Monarch of the Forest, may dear-deer-God help you and support you in everything you do.'

Once again everyone present grunted and tweeted and made noises in their own way. Then I stood on the high rock and gave a short grunt-speech. Twig radio took the whole grunt-speech down in short-beak to transmit to all Staglands.

After I had finished, there was more grunting and tweeting, and then the head stag policeman got on his hind legs and grunted for three cheer-grunts and tweets for the new Monarch. The noise was deafening.

At that moment three Jumbos flew across with booful vapour trails, and I looked up and thought of little Stag-Jesus and the old Monarch and Ronnie's half brother, and the old switch policeman, and Jeannie's Mummy and Tollie Trout's brother, and Father Christmas with his reindeer, and the many, many other peoples of all sorts who were up there.

And while I was thinking about all these peoples, Rory and several of his friends did the most beautiful horn-dance you have ever seen, to the music at the beginning of *Stagland of Hope and Glory*, and then, Henry, and then the jog-trot past started. It was oh so wonderful. The huge twee-grunt choir stood in front of me and twee-grunted:

> Stag-Land of hope and glory,
> Forests of the free,
> Keep our Island's story
> Safe for you and me
> Higher and still Higher, let the Jumbos fly,
> We will join our friends there, one day in the sky,
> Till then we hope to serve thee,
> And help to keep thee free.

*... Professor, New Monarch and New Chamberlain ...*

I stood on my rock with the new Lord-Stag-Chamber-Lain, Rory and Jeannie, while hundreds and hundreds of stag-peoples jogged past, led by the head stag-policeman. Then the hind herds followed, and I saw Morag and her new twins (they seemed to leave the procession after they had passed me), then the Roe deer, led by Ronnie and Mona, and then the hares and the bunnies and the birds and King Swallow, who had come all the way back from the south for the occasion, and Gorkie with Miss Partridge, and Olly and Roger and so many others.

There was a small gap before Mr MacTavish appeared with Hamish and Trash, wagging his tail, and Fergie with his two ponies and then the head-horrible-keeper-hunter. Right at the end, the two two-legged nobbers who had fallen into the loch marched past smartly at the salute, dressed in their Cub-Scout uniforms.

When they had all gone, one last rather ageing figure came round the side of the mound on my right, very slowly and with much dignity. It was Professor Red Deer. He came up to me, bowed low, wagged his tail, paused, gave me a wonderful smile and then walked off, followed by the choir.

I felt a nudge by my right side. Morag and her twin baby nobbers were beside me, and Morag was lick-polishing my side. There was another nudge on the other side and more lick-polishing; this was Trash who had left the procession and run back to be with me.

Chamber-Lain and Rory jogged off after giving a little bow. A moment later Trash gave a wuff and trotted off, wagging his tail. Then Morag gave me a big lick on the nose and went away with her twins and Jeannie whom she had promised to look after. She now had three babies to look after, Henry, and she was looking after a hind baby for the first time.

I, The Monarch, was all on my own now – quite alone, except for my six special smell-sentries. It was then that I realised that Top People are nearly always quite alone, Henry, except for dear-deer-God who stays by their side.

And then I woke up.

Henry, you may have heard the expression 'dreams come true' – well on Church-day this dream did come true. My real Monarch-ation was almost exactly the same as my dream, but the weather wasn't quite as nice.

Very sadly, I have to stop writing to you now, Henry, and devote all my time to looking after Stagland. We have loved writing our weekly letters throughout the past year, and I hope you have enjoyed getting them. We look forward to seeing you and your Mum and your Dad and your Granny and your Grandpa in Mull very often in the years ahead. It is an Island we love, and we believe you love it too as well as loving all those who live here.

Be a good boy and work hard and play hard,

Your devoted Pal

Alby

P. S. Next week you will get a copy of the grunt-speech to the folk of Stagland which I made at my Monarch-ation – by special delivery and, sadly, that will be the last.

# Letter No. 1 *from Golden Eagle Post to Henry*

## (52 from Mull)

TELEPHONE:
Grr 2

THE MYXIE GARAGE PO
ISLE OF MULL
ARGYLL
SCOTLAND
13th February

Grrr, Henry, Grrr, Grrr,

This is Golden Eagle Postie. I promised Alby, Monarch of the Forest, that I would deliver a copy of the grunt-speech that he gave to his people of Stagland on the occasion of his Monarch-ation last week.

It was a very good grunt-speech, Henry. We all listened very carefully. The deer and all the other animals sat on their bottoms with their front legs crossed. Twig radio members either glided overhead or sat on birch branches behind The Monarch. There was no wind, just sun and frost. All was silent except for the faint trickling of the Mossieburn in the distance. This is what the Monarch grunted:

'Friends of Stagland, four-legged and two-legged, I am proud to have been appointed Monarch of the Forest, and I will do all I can to help you have happy and useful times here.

'I believe that Stagland Forest belongs to all of us. This is where we were born. This is where we feed. This is where we play. And this is where we will die.

'I do not mean we must not welcome visitors; we must; because only in that way can they enjoy our hills and learn about our peoples.

'We will try to teach visitors not to make horrible messes with their tinfoil and apple cores. Many of them think a skivvy stag comes round with a stag rover every two hours collecting their mess.

'We like visitors who want to love our hills and understand us.

'We will defend ourselves from those townie visitors who have not been trained in the ways of Stagland and only come here to shoot our people.

'Yet we have to understand that if our numbers are not kept down by the horrible hunters and the sausage machines, there will be too many of us and we will not have enough food to grow booful heads anymore.

'Whatever herd you belong to, I ask you to be friends together and help me to help you to keep the Mulloch Stagland the happiest place under the Flying Jumbos.'

That is all he said, Henry. I know he thinks of you and your Mum and Dad very often, and I know that he hopes you will be a good boy at this time because his horns will be getting loose again soon, and you will remember that as long as you are a good boy, his loose horns don't hurt. Alby told you about that fifty-two weeks ago – last time his horns were loose – remember?

So be a good boy for Alby's sake.

This is my last delivery to your home, Henry and it brings with it very best Stagland love and wishes.

Your old Postie,

# *Grrr*